AN ALIEN COLLECTIVE

by

Roxanne Barbour

WEE CREEK PRESS
www.weecreekpress.com

Diane
The Future is Yours!

Roxanne Barbour

Published by
WEE CREEK PRESS
An Imprint of
WHISKEY CREEK PRESS
PO Box 51052
Casper, WY 82605-1052
www.whiskeycreekpress.com

Copyright 2014 by Roxanne Barbour

Warning: The unauthorized reproduction or distribution of this copyrighted work is illegal. Criminal copyright infringement, including infringement without monetary gain, is investigated by the FBI and is punishable by up to 5 (five) years in federal prison and a fine of $250,000.

Names, characters and incidents depicted in this book are products of the author's imagination or are used fictitiously. Any resemblance to actual events, locales, organizations, or persons, living or dead, is entirely coincidental and beyond the intent of the author or the publisher.

No part of this book may be reproduced or transmitted in any form or by any means, electronic or mechanical, including photocopying, recording, or by any information storage and retrieval system, without permission in writing from the publisher.

Ebook ISBN: 978-1-61160-927-1
Print ISBN: 978-1-61160-993-6

**Cover Artist: Molly Courtright
Editor: Rick Reisinger
Interior Design: Jim Brown
Printed in the United States of America**

Dedication

To my husband, Norm, and to my parents, who always believed I could do anything I set my mind to do.

Chapter 1

I opened my eyes and gagged. I discovered I was lying face down, and that my mouth was wide open to the grass beneath me. I lifted my head, rolled my body to the right, and sat up.
Where am I?
An unfamiliar environment greeted me.
To get a better view of my surroundings, I stood up and took a couple of stiff and hesitant steps. Then I stopped. A small enclosed compound surrounded me, and I was not alone. About six or seven other young adults were slowly getting to their feet or starting to move about. Few words were being spoken; the others seemed as stunned as I was.
My head is killing me!
The compound we were in was enclosed by a metal fence and carpeted with grass. The sunshine glinted off the six foot high, mesh-like fence. Some sort of large box occupied one corner. To add to my confusion, the sun seemed as strange as the purple-hued grass.

An Alien Collective – Roxanne Barbour

Thinking I could get a better view of the area, I walked towards the fence where it connected to the corner box.

What's this?

My mind froze in confusion, and I found myself a little breathless.

Over the top of the box, I looked into an adjacent compound inhabited by some strange beings. The humanoids were unlike anything I'd ever seen. These aliens appeared to have all the same body parts as we did, but that's where any resemblance stopped. Their baldness and large ears seemed to complement their dark mottled skin. They had a tall, slim physique. My appearance had instantly stopped their restless movement.

One being was close to my location. Neither of us moved as we stared intently at each other over the top of the box.

The alien's clothing appeared to be soft, supple, and camouflaging. Our closeness allowed me to observe that his skin was consistent with his clothing.

It was unnerving how the alien was similarly undressing me. I felt like I was on display—the feeling was probably mutual.

"Where are they from?" I mumbled out loud.

"We are from the planet Temma," the alien answered.

Instinctively, I took a big step backward. Then I grunted when I stumbled and almost landed on my ass. I needed to get a handle on my reactions.

"You speak English?"

An Alien Collective – Roxanne Barbour

"Unlikely. But take a look at what is around your neck." The alien lifted an upper appendage—very similar to a hand—and pointed at me.

In my confusion, I hadn't noticed an object hanging on a cord around my neck. I reached up and grabbed it. A small black metal object with lights, numbers, and letters on its surface occupied my hand.

"I believe we've all been given universal translators."

"Who are you?" I blurted. I don't know why that popped out of my mouth.

"As I said, I am a Temman male, and my name is Stire."

I should respond, I thought.

"Oh, ah, ah, my name is Cyn. Actually, Cyn-Tia Silverthorne, but just call me Cyn. And I am a girl, I mean female, of the human species."

Get a grip, idiot. That sounded really stilted.

"Where are we? What are we doing here? Did you bring us here?" I stammered. By this time, the rest of the humans had gathered behind me.

I tried to read Stire's body language and facial expressions, but my senses were currently overloaded.

Unexpectedly, Stire thrust his hand towards me. Startled, I put my hand on the box between us to steady myself.

A harsh beep erupted from the box, and I jumped. The loud sound made both of us take a closer look. About eight feet on a side, no distinguishing marks were visible on the large closed container.

Looking around, I discovered there were four

An Alien Collective – Roxanne Barbour

fenced compounds accessible to the box—one compound for each of the races: human, Temman, and two new alien species.

Stire stood in front of the box where it protruded into his compound. As brave, or as foolish as I, he reached out to touch it himself. We both heard a similar sound to the first.

At the second loud beep, the remainder of the inhabitants of the compounds started walking warily toward the central box. An alien from one of the remaining two compounds touched the box and received the same sound.

Nothing happened; we just stared at each other.

Enough of this inaction!

"You, touch the box!" I said as I pointed at the closest alien from the remaining compound.

There was no response for a moment. After a pause, an apparently female alien responded.

"Why should I do what you say? We Irandi do not cooperate with strangers."

And I bet we are very strange to them!

Before I had a chance to respond, Stire interjected, "Although I do not know what is going on, I do not believe that any of us caused this situation. So we will have to cooperate—at least to the extent of gathering information." He paused, then said, "At the moment, someone from each of three compounds has touched this box and nothing has happened, except for the beeps. So, I think someone from your compound should also touch the box."

An Alien Collective – Roxanne Barbour

"Maybe the fourth could be anyone?" the Irandi responded.

Stire gestured to another Temman. When the second Temman touched the box, nothing was heard.

We all looked at the Irandi that had spoken. After a moment's hesitation, she reluctantly touched an appendage to the box.

A fourth beep was heard, and a package spewed out onto my feet. From the movements of the other aliens, they had obviously also received something.

The lizard-like Irandi was the first to pick up its package. Nothing happened, so my fear of a bomb was unfounded; although, thinking back later, that notion wasn't very logical.

The other three of us retrieved our own packages. Mine contained a few pages covered in writing, so I started to read. I had never been able to resist reading anything put in front of me.

"Cyn, are your notes written in your own language?" Stire asked.

"Yes, they are. And yours?"

"Indeed they are, and my notes say to confer with my own people and discuss the contents of the package."

If I could read an alien, this one was looking confused. The other two were holding their packages as far in front of themselves as they could, and that reeked of uncertainty.

I had no argument with them; I desperately needed a little information about our predicament, too.

An Alien Collective — Roxanne Barbour

"Why don't we gather with our own people and discuss what we've found. We could meet back here in a little while?" I suggested. I assumed the differing physical gestures made by the aliens were their forms of showing assent because they quickly walked away.

I turned around and wandered towards the far corner of the human compound. As I proceeded, I gathered up the other humans. I sat down in the corner and looked around; we were definitely not on Earth. I didn't know where we were, or how we got here. I picked up my papers and started to read, but voices intruded.

"What's happening? Where are we?"

"What's in the package?"

"What are those other beings? Are they aliens?"

The voices overlapped and were a little hysterical.

After I raised my hand, quiet eventually descended on the group. I quickly counted. There were eight of us, and we all appeared to be older teenagers.

"I have no information yet; let me read these notes. Perhaps the answers are in here." I started to organize the papers on my lap.

"Don't keep anything from us," said a fairly tall, dark skinned guy, shaking his short brown hair.

Irritated, I looked up. "I'm going to read these papers out loud, as I said before."

"My name is Hamza, and you did not say you were going to read everything to us."

A couple of people hushed him. To diffuse the situation, I decided it was a good time to introduce ourselves to each other. There were four females and four

An Alien Collective – Roxanne Barbour

males in our group, and we appeared to be from different backgrounds. *Is this an important fact?*

After the introductions, the humans settled down again.

"Ok, the first note in this package is the instruction to go back and read and discuss all of the following items with everyone else in your group. So that's what I'm doing." I tried not to sound annoyed with Hamza. "There are ten items. Let me just read all of them out loud, then we can discuss each item separately.

"1. We have brought you here, from your home planet, for a reason. The reason will not be revealed at this time.

"2. You will be living and working in an integrated village with the other species.

"3. The four people who each received this package will form your Managing Committee. The members of this committee cannot be changed. Their DNA is necessary to open the supply box.

"4. The Managing Committee will receive instructions and supplies each morning. The Managing Committee will be your government.

"5. Today's instructions and supplies are waiting in the supply box.

"6. Around your neck is a universal translator, which also incorporates a timepiece and a recording device.

"7. There is clothing and footwear for each individual in the supply box. Discard your old clothing.

"8. Do not attempt to leave. There is nowhere to go.

"9. Discuss your situation for a few moments.
"10. Then the Managing Committee must meet at the supply box."

I dropped the list in my lap and tried to breathe a little slower. My confusion was escalating—I had just woken up with no clue about my situation, and now I was in charge? From the stunned looks on the faces in front of me, I gathered the others were all experiencing the same shock.

All of a sudden I was in a strange place, part of a managing committee and dealing with numerous strange beings, and who knew what else would be thrown at me. And there appeared to be no way to go home.

"This isn't fair. I want to go back to Earth," said a green-eyed girl. The force with which she brushed her red, curly hair out of her face said enough. "I never thought that abduction by aliens would be part of my life."

Janet Kahn's statement nailed our predicament and forced me, at least temporarily, to stop feeling sorry for myself.

"Janet, it does seem pretty rotten. My major concern is the *why* of the situation. Why are we here? We don't even know *who* brought us here." I paused for a moment. "I'm guessing it's another type of alien we haven't met yet." The number of different aliens in our current situation was overwhelming; although, on another level, it was quite exciting!

Hamza brought me back to earth—actually, that expression didn't quite fit.

An Alien Collective – Roxanne Barbour

"I don't understand why you're on the Managing Committee; I should be on it. I am in charge of many programs on Earth," he said.

Although I thought Hamza was exactly the wrong person to be on a *committee*, I decided to be tactful. "Perhaps you should be, but I don't see how we can change anything. These instructions are pretty explicit." I pointed to the sheets in my lap.

Hamza just pursed his lips.

"There's nothing else in this envelope, so it doesn't look like we're going to get any more insights at the moment." I had started to put the instructions back in the envelope when Jack approached me.

"Cyn, I'm a journalism student, and I was wondering if I could get those papers. We should start a journal on what's happened to all of us. And since these gadgets are apparently recording devices too, I thought I would record these instructions."

It wasn't actually such a bad idea.

"Good idea. I'll give them to you a little later; I need them for now. But take this envelope; you can also be our archivist. Who knows what the future holds? Maybe we'll all write our memoirs." I couldn't bring myself to smile.

I continued, "It's time for me to meet the rest of the managing committee."

With that comment, we all walked to the supply box.

Chapter 2

The supply box was quite a popular spot. The rest of the managing committee waited there for me. I recognized Stire, but I wasn't sure about the other two.

A few steps back, the remainder of the abductees hovered in groups in their compounds. It occurred to me that everyone was looking anxious and upset, but perhaps those were just my own feelings.

The four of us, the managing committee, studied each other for a moment.

"Stire, could I see your instructions? I just want to see what your language looks like," I said to break the ice.

Stire and I traded. I flipped through his sheets of paper—although I wasn't even sure if the sheets were made from paper. His written characters were very unusual.

The other two beings silently joined in our exchange.

After a few moments of looking over the various

An Alien Collective – Roxanne Barbour

sheets of instructions, Stire said, "Cyn, we should all introduce ourselves, as it appears we'll be working closely together."

I had to agree with Stire. From what I could glean from our instructions, we had a lot to do.

"Ok, I'll start. My name is Cyn-Tia Silverthorne, but just call me Cyn. I am from a planet called Earth. Parts of Earth are similar to the little I have seen so far of this planet, but I don't think this is Earth. For one thing, the sun and ground cover are slightly different. What else? Oh, yes. I am a female of my species, and I am seventeen years old. Seventeen is equivalent to a teenager, or a young adult. I'm studying mathematics and computer science at school." For the time being, they didn't need any more information about me.

Next, Stire held up his hand. "I am Stire. You may call me Stire." I suspected Stire was trying out a little Temman humor. "I am from a planet called Temma. My age is five, but I believe it is equivalent to Cyn's age. And I am male. Most of our planet is very dry, and certainly does not have anywhere near this amount of vegetation. I am currently studying chemistry, and I will shortly be moving to study water preservation." He sighed. "I hope."

Silence enveloped the four of us for a moment or two while we thought about our predicament.

Then an alien, with mauve skin slightly darker than the others of its species, began to speak.

While it spoke, a large raised band of flesh around its head appeared to move a little. "My name is Frakis a

An Alien Collective – Roxanne Barbour

Kirba. I am from a planet called Reanno. Our planet would be classified as a water planet. Everywhere you look, you see water. So, Reanno is distinctly unlike Temma and this planet. We have a matriarchal society, and I am female."

Frakis hesitated for a moment. "The Kirba in my name indicates which clan I belong to. We have four clans: Kirba, Camp, Simo, and Brewst. Normally, we call each other by our whole name, but I will make an exception in this place. You may call me Frakis. I am sixteen, which appears to be about equivalent to everyone else's age." The band around Frakis's head seemed to settle down.

Frakis certainly gave me something to think about. I wondered what she studied. Perhaps the Reannone didn't have a formal educational system.

The last member of our committee spoke. It was the Irandi we had forced to touch the supply box. The Irandi was humanoid, but shaped like an upright lizard with yellow eyes and twelve fingers. "I am called Tine Jana. Tine is also a clan name. We have many clans; although only four appear to be represented here. Our planet is called Irandis. And, again, it is unlike our current location. Irandis is mostly tropical forest. Calling me Jana is correct. I have thirteen years, and I am female. We consider ourselves young adults at this age." Jana stopped talking and stepped back.

No one said a word, so I decided to babble. "This is so exciting. Never, in my wildest dreams, did I imagine that I would meet real aliens; people that look and act

An Alien Collective – Roxanne Barbour

so differently. All the stories I read never prepared me for this moment!" I sighed. "On the other hand, I certainly miss my family and friends. Don't take this the wrong way, but I wish I was home on Earth." My smile had disappeared.

While I was talking, I had gradually noticed Stire looking at me with some speculation. I wondered what he was thinking about, or if I was even reading him correctly.

Stire spoke. "Since we four have become the managing committee, through no decision of our own, we must learn to discuss everything. We should have meetings every day; there will be much to plan. For our first action, we must open the supply box; we need to see our new instructions. Perhaps there will be some clues as to why we're here. I must reiterate that we Temmans are upset we've been abducted."

"Join the club," I murmured.

"What does 'join the club' mean?" asked Frakis. "Isn't a club used to hit something?"

"You're right. In our language, club does mean an instrument to hit something, but it also means a group of people joined together for some specific purpose." I smiled. "These universal translators apparently are not perfect. What I was trying to say was that we all seem to be reacting in the same way."

"Let's get this box open," interrupted Stire.

I looked all over the portion of the supply box visible to me. Each quarter of the box top seemed to have an indentation. I noticed nothing else.

An Alien Collective — Roxanne Barbour

Frakis said, "Let's each put an appendage, or a hand, or whatever you call them, in our respective indents."

"Were these indentations here before? I don't remember them."

No one else did either. It looked like our original touches had changed the top of the box.

We all reached out; Jana was the last to put her hand on the top. At that point, the top of the supply box split open and started to slide down into its sides. I was startled and pulled my hand back. Shortly afterwards, the fences retracted into the ground. Apparently, there was no longer any need for a delineation of our compounds.

The supply box was stuffed full. There were sheets of paper and plastic wrapped clothing on the top layer, and numerous boxes underneath.

The managing committee sorted through the instructions to get to the ones we each could decipher, and then we started to read.

During the time it took to read our new instructions, I glanced up and noticed that, even though the fences were down, no one in the compounds was moving.

In a moment, Stire commented, "This is pretty much what I expected. It looks like the first thing we do is take everything from the supply box and rendezvous at the cookhouse. Our abductors have given us a map of some of the areas in this settlement, or the *village,* as they call it. The map shows us how to find the cookhouse, so we should go there first. Then we can sit

An Alien Collective – Roxanne Barbour

down and study the rest of our instructions."

No one argued with Stire's firm statement, so we proceeded to organize our own people to each grab a box or two. There were a lot of items in the supply box, and I looked forward to seeing what we had received. With such differing species, some of the items should prove to be fascinating.

With Stire in the lead, the group proceeded along the path looking like a flock of birds with their heads bobbing about taking in the sights. The surrounding countryside was mostly invisible because of the low rise buildings all around us.

All of a sudden, I found myself on the ground; I had been pushed from behind.

I heard Jack yelling, "Why did you knock her down?"

Janet helped me to my feet, and I saw that Jack had grabbed the arm of a Temman. They struggled for a moment, but Jack wouldn't let go.

"What is going on?" demanded Stire. The word had apparently reached him at the head of the line.

"This idiot pushed Cyn to the ground," said Jack.

"Are you ok?" Stire asked me, in a quieter voice.

"Just a little scrape on my hand." It really wasn't much; it was the shock of being pushed that had me upset.

Stire glared at the Temman. "I am sorry about this. I will take care of the situation," he said to me. Stire made a gesture to the other Temman and said, "Come with me."

An Alien Collective – Roxanne Barbour

We watched the two of them walk to the head of the line.

Is this my future?

The cookhouse was close to our starting point: Awakening Square. The outside of the single story building was clad with gray colored boards. Inside, we found a cooking area, an open dining area, cooking equipment, and stacked tables and chairs.

We piled everything from the supply box in the middle of the open room, and then the committee huddled together to decide our next actions.

"It looks like we need to assign housing and clothing," said Jana.

I had studied the map and instructions. "Apparently, each housing unit is to contain one Human, one Irandi, one Temman, and one Reannone. And one of the housing units is specifically labeled for us." We were all bent over studying our notes.

"The Irandi will not be happy with this arrangement. We should make each housing unit uni-species," said Jana.

Not very friendly!

"Jana, I believe it would be foolish to disobey our abductors at this early stage of our captivity. Let them think we are obedient until we have gathered a goodly amount of information," said Frakis. "Here's what I suggest. Let's pile all the clothing together in one area. Then we'll give every person a set of clothing and tell each of them which unit they'll be housed in."

"Apparently we can record with our universal trans-

An Alien Collective – Roxanne Barbour

lators. Has anyone figured out how to do that?" I asked.

"I think notes on the housing assignments would be useful." Little did I know it would turn out to be an invaluable suggestion. In just a few moments, Frakis became the first to decipher the art of recording with her universal translator.

"There is also a toiletries pack for each person. Hopefully, they are species specific," Stire added. "They should be given out at the same time as the clothing and shoe packages."

There was chaos for a while, especially when trying to determine the clothing sizes, but we eventually sorted it out and sent everyone on their way.

Our housing unit was located next to both the cookhouse and Awakening Square. It was a one level building covered with brown paneling. Our abductors didn't seem to like bright colors.

Our unit contained four bedrooms, a sitting area, and a bathroom. Each bedroom had a planet name written in its own characters. Obviously, our rooms were going to be slightly different to take into account our differing physiologies.

My bedroom was sparsely furnished. Besides a bed, with linens, the room contained shelving, a bench, and what appeared to be a lamp sitting on the window ledge. I dropped my new clothes on the bed and sat down on the bench. The monstrosity of my situation engulfed me; the tears rolled down my face. I was having a meltdown.

Will I ever see my family again?

After a few moments of despair, I gave myself a little shake, and then changed my clothes. Knowing I needed a freshening, I wandered to the bathroom. Quite unique—our abductors had managed to make uni-species fixtures.

Shortly, all four of us met in the sitting area. Our new clothing fit well because the dark colored shirts and pants had numerous ways for making adjustments. Most of the adjustments could be made by Velcro-like tabs, but there was also a belt on the pants and a built-in drawstring on the shirt. The sandals only had Velcro tabs. They were comfortable, but they felt like heavy duty walking shoes.

"This clothing is quite practical for everyone," commented Frakis. A bright red scarf adorned her neck.

"Why are you wearing a scarf?" I asked.

"The scarf signifies our clan. It's tradition to wear one."

"Why?" asked Jana.

"I'm not completely sure; it's mostly historical. We used to have many clan wars, so we needed a way to tell the clans apart. We have worn them for so long that we feel essentially naked if we aren't wearing one." It certainly spiced up her clothing. I would have to think of something for myself. I noticed Jana, the Irandi, had jewelry on her fingers.

"Let's not waste any more time. We need to get back to the cookhouse; a lot of work is waiting," said Stire.

The next item on the agenda we had received was to assign tasks to everyone.

An Alien Collective – Roxanne Barbour

According to our instructions, we needed to unpack and store the contents of the remaining boxes, find a supply of wood somewhere in the village for the cook stoves, set up the tables and chairs, and start the first meal.
This is a lot to be accomplished on the first day.
"The Irandi are concerned about this whole situation," said Jana. "How long are we supposed to stay here? I know we don't know why we're here, but wouldn't knowing the length of our stay help us plan?"
"It certainly would," replied Stire. "But let's think about it later. We're not going to get any answers from our abductors today. Right now, we need to get working on our projects." He seemed a little pushy.
"Does anyone know what time of day it is?" I asked.
"Why?" quizzed Frakis.
"Since we have timepieces, we should set them to our best estimate. Then we can plan our mealtimes, and such."
"How do we know how many hours are in a day? Or even if this planet has days?" asked Jana.
"We don't know anything for sure. But I would guess we were given timepieces because we do have a night and day, so we could synchronize everyone," I said.
"Well, my best guess is mid-afternoon," suggested Stire. "So, if we guess at a twenty-five hour day, it's about 'fifteen-hours' now." There were no objections. "I am sure we will have to make many more adjust-

ments, and not only our timepieces, as we gather data," he added. "But we've gotten off track. We need to organize our tasks."

"Our first project should be to assign some people to look for the woodpile. We're going to need a meal soon," said Frakis.

"Yes, and let's discuss a meal schedule later. I'm sure we all have different routines."

I continued, "From what I have observed, we have thirty-two people here; eight from each species." Apparently we could all count; no one voiced any disagreement. "So, why don't we send eight to gather the wood; I'm sure it won't be far. Then maybe we could have eight cooks and helpers; perhaps another six to unpack these boxes, with another six to start setting up the chairs and tables and helping with the unpacking. That leaves the four of us to go back to Awakening Square and take a better look around. We probably missed some clues or other important information in the initial confusion."

Some clues would be nice!

"What is 'Awakening Square'?" asked Jana.

"Oh, sorry, that's just my own name for where we woke up."

"Actually, it's an excellent name," commented Frakis. "And I have no objections to your suggestions about the duty splits. We need to start somewhere."

So that's what we did. There was a lot of grumbling but it seemed good-natured, for the most part. A state of shock still permeated the atmosphere.

An Alien Collective – Roxanne Barbour

We helped with some of the unpacking, so we had a better idea of what supplies we had, and then we walked over to Awakening Square. This time, we took a closer look at our surroundings. Studying the area had not been foremost in our minds the first time we'd been here.

Awakening Square was near the edge of our village. As a result, we had a good view of the countryside. In the distance, there were tall mountains covered with snow. Surrounding the village were acres of lush fields. I couldn't see a water source, but the fields would need one close by. Just a hint of scent was evident.

We wandered around Awakening Square for a bit, studying the details.

"I'm trying to figure out a reason for us being here, but nothing comes to mind. This whole situation is obviously well-planned, but why? It seems strange to throw together four wildly differing species. It can't be a random happening." Stire sounded a little unsure of himself, and that was the first time I had heard that from him.

"We must be involved in some kind of experiment. Some advanced species brought us here so they could study us. And they must be advanced, because this is certainly not my planet, and we have not developed any way to get here ourselves. On the other hand, maybe one of your species abducted the other three of us!" barked Jana, throwing her arms in the air.

Jana was losing her grip on reality. Not a surprise.

An Alien Collective — Roxanne Barbour

"Jana, if one of our species did this, why would we be here too?" I asked. I was trying to be reasonable. "Honestly, we only have space travel to neighboring planets in our solar system, and even that's only in an early exploratory stage."

"And we regularly travel to one other planet in our system, but we haven't developed out-of-system travel," added Stire.

"And we're thinking about it," said Frakis, with what I assumed was a smile.

So the other species aren't any more developed than we are. What are the chances of four species, being at the same stage of development, landing in the same situation?

This was something to think about.

"So, to summarize: we've all been brought here from different planets for some unknown reason, and by some unknown race." I took a deep breath. "That's not much data, and certainly not very comforting."

"No, it's not. And we haven't found any clues. The only item of interest is the supply box. Does anyone think it works both ways? If we put something in it, will the item disappear?" Stire asked.

We walked over to the supply box and looked inside. I couldn't see any indication of machinery or electronics. It looked like nothing more than a large empty wooden box.

Frakis took off her scarf and said, "Here, let's put this in the box and see what happens."

"Don't you need it?" I asked.

An Alien Collective – Roxanne Barbour

"I'll be fine. I have my clan belt." I hadn't noticed Frakis was wearing her own red belt. Apparently, she had not told us everything about clan customs.

So we put the scarf in the box and closed it up. We waited a few moments and then looked back inside. The scarf was still there.

"Maybe we need to leave the scarf in the box until the next time we get our supplies. Perhaps the supply box can only be operated from the other end?" said Jana.

"That's not a bad plan. Let's leave it where it is until tomorrow," I replied. "Has anyone discovered any clues to help us?"

There was no response, and I hadn't expected one. Awakening Square was devoid of any distinguishing characteristics. Our abductors were not going to be that unsophisticated. We continued to study the area, but it was fruitless. We needed to move on.

"Ok, let's do a little exploring away from the village. Which direction should we go?" I asked.

"Let's go north," said Jana, as she pointed towards the mountains.

"How do you know where north is?" Stire asked.

"I can tell by the sun."

No one argued with her. Did it really matter what the direction was labeled?

We walked north, away from the village. The landscape consisted of low lying fields and some short shrubbery. A slight tinge of purple continued to enhance the greenery.

An Alien Collective – Roxanne Barbour

After about fifteen minutes of walking north, we changed our direction to circle the village. Shortly, we came upon a path that led away from the village; probably the equivalent of west. The path was quite wide, but there was no indication it had ever been used.

"Let's take this path," said Jana. "It must lead somewhere." She seemed quite the explorer.

"Actually, I think we should go back to the cookhouse and see what's happening. We need to keep everything organized and under control," Frakis said.

Jana took one look at us and, without a word, stomped off towards the village. We watched her go.

Frakis sighed. "This managing committee is excellent experience for me, since I'm studying city administration. Or I was…" Frakis looked a little crestfallen after her remark.

"Good thoughts," said Stire.

I wasn't sure if Stire meant Frakis had a good plan, or if she needed to think positively. Either way, Frakis seemed to perk up a little. The three of us started walking in the direction of the cookhouse. We were just a short distance behind Jana.

Back at the cookhouse, some progress had been made. Most of the tables and chairs had been assembled and set up. From where we were standing in the dining area, the kitchen area seemed chaotic, but the smell of smoke indicated the stoves had been lit.

The committee walked into the kitchen. A door on the back wall opened, and Jack appeared with a load of wood. He dumped it by a stove.

"Where did you find the wood?" I asked.

"It was piled right beside a store room we found not very far away." Jack grinned. "My curiosity got the better of me, and I took a peek inside. The store room is stuffed with all sorts of articles. There are things like wheelbarrows, gardening tools, coils of wire and rope, and many other items. Some of them look quite alien."

I smiled. "Some of them may be native to our new friends."

"Or maybe whoever brought us here." A faraway look appeared in his eyes for a few seconds, and then he snapped back. "I've made a mental list of all the topics I want to write about; all of the experiences we have undergone today. And, to top it off, this store room excites me. I don't know why!"

"Well, just remember to write it all down. You have an important job to do." I decided to change the subject. "How much wood is there?"

"Probably enough for a couple of days. We'll have to see how fast the cooks use it up, but I think we'll probably need more pretty soon. We're creating a stockpile outside the cookhouse. And we found some tarps in the store room, in case it rains. We have no idea what the weather patterns are like."

"Agreed. We don't know much of anything yet, but I'll put a source of wood on our to-do list."

Jack took off to get another load of wood, and I turned back to the kitchen. Stire was listening to a discussion. The stances of the participants indicated a disagreement. I walked a little closer.

An Alien Collective – Roxanne Barbour

"I am not going to let some alien watch me cook our food. Cooking is a private matter. We have many rituals we perform while we cook. It is part of our religion," said an Irandi.

"That is indeed a problem," agreed Stire. He looked at me. *Was I supposed to come up with an answer?* Probably, since the other cook involved was a human.

I thought for a moment.

"We need four areas in the kitchen so food can be prepared for each species, and the kitchen looks like it has been set up that way. Why don't you take one of the end stations? Most of the cooks will not be near you. And we'll try to rig up some kind of divider on the other side of your station—that way no one will watch you. Since we need a meal shortly, it's probably best you all get started." The Irandi cook acted somewhat mollified. I may not have been entirely convincing, but the cooks did turn away and get back to work.

I gestured Stire aside. "There is so much we haven't thought about. It's mind boggling. For example, how many meals a day does everyone need? Most humans have three main meals, and two or three snacks. We need to set up a meal schedule that accommodates all species."

"Yes, we do."

So Stire and I gathered up Jana and Frakis and worked out a meal schedule. Of course, we did have to make some assumptions about our new world.

In the end, it turned out three meals a day would work. The Irandi normally had two meals a day, so they would snack with us during the midday meal. Three meals a day was the norm for the rest of us.

A long countertop had been installed between the seating area and the cooking facilities. When the cooks were finished with their preparations, the dishes of food were piled along the countertop, and everyone helped themselves. The dining area contained plenty of space for everyone to be comfortable dining.

Jana stood up and let out what sounded to me like a shriek. The dining area was immediately silent.

"I'm sure not everyone follows a religion, and certainly not mine. However, I would just like to say something." She paused for a couple of seconds. Then she held out her hands, bowed her head, and said, "Blessings on everyone, blessings on this food, and hopeful blessings our situation will resolve." At the end of her blessing, she slowly dropped into her chair.

I heard a few murmurs—prayers perhaps—then everyone began to eat. We, the managing committee, had a table to ourselves.

"Does anyone know how this universal translator works? Most of the time, I hear the translation quite clearly. But why don't I hear the original words and the translation all jumbled up together?" Although I happily accepted the universal translator, curiosity made me ask.

Jana suggested an answer. "I'm studying astronomy, but I have to confess I'm also addicted to 'scientification'."

"What's that?"

An Alien Collective – Roxanne Barbour

"Oh, fiction with wild scientific speculation thrown in." Jana looked a little flushed.

"We call that science fiction," I added, with a smile.

"Well, anyway, I found a theory about universal translators which says they tune directly into the frequency of your brain, so you don't get any confusion. Perhaps that's how these ones work. It is satisfying that they work. I don't know how we could get anything accomplished, otherwise."

No one could argue with her statement.

The dining area attracted my attention. "Has anyone noticed that a lot of the tables are only occupied by a single species?"

"It's a natural reaction to the stress we're all feeling. Everyone needs to find some comfort in familiarity. Our lives, right now, are filled with uncertainty," commented Frakis.

All four of us continued to study the dining area, but no one else commented.

To change the topic, I asked, "Our abductors seem to have supplied all the basic necessities. Any thoughts about the housing units?"

"They seem a little sparse, but at least they are suited to the Irandi needs," commented Jana. "Especially the bathroom. Our abductors have ingeniously figured out a way to make a bathroom usable by everyone. Having a couple of facilities in the cookhouse is also appreciated."

Stire spoke up. "We have clothing that is quite

An Alien Collective – Roxanne Barbour

practical. Although only three sizes were available, the availability of adjustments makes the clothing workable. Since such an elaborate setup has been created for us, I believe we're going to be here for a considerable length of time. So, we're going to need a continual supply of food and more than one set of clothing. And, in particular, we're going to need a means of cleaning items."

I added my thoughts. "That has also been planned for. I talked to the cooks and we have hot and cold running water in the kitchen."

"I briefly checked out the bathroom facilities in our housing unit. Hot and cold water was installed there also," said Jana.

"So we have the means to clean clothes and dishes. Of course, we don't know where the hot water is coming from, and I've not seen any power sources. But we've only been here a few hours; there is so much to learn."

I was feeling a little weary, so I said, "I don't know about the rest of you, but I'm fading. It may be whatever they drugged us with, or I might be over stimulated, but I should probably get an early night."

"Yes, I'm also tired, but we need to become familiar with our new home. Why don't we suggest that everyone takes a short leisurely stroll around the village to relax and explore, and then settle down for the night?" Frakis had a comforting nature.

"Before we do anything, we should decide on the kitchen cleanup," said Jana. "The Irandi will not be the only ones doing dishes." She seemed irritated; perhaps her species did things a little differently.

In the end, the easiest solution was to alternate the daily cleanup amongst the races. Tonight's toss fell to the Irandi. Jana stood up to offer a protest, but then she backed off.

Various groupings, mostly non-mixed, took off from the cookhouse when their meals ended. A stroll was a welcome way to aid in digestion.

I had perked up a bit, so I joined the managing committee and we walked north again.

Even though it felt like evening to me, the light level remained quite high. It was going to be interesting to see what the length of the day eventually turned out to be.

We discovered a stream on our stroll. The wide shallow water course rushed past us. Because of the meadows lapping the stream, we easily walked along the edge. We also discovered a piping system that took water from the stream in the general direction of our village. The source of our cold water had been found.

The exercise had given me a little more energy, and since a little more planning was necessary, we decided to return to the cookhouse. On our walk back, we encountered a few groups still exploring, but the majority of our populace also appeared to be headed back to the cookhouse.

The cleanup crew had put a few items out for an evening snack. The cooks had helped the Irandi so they would know what was appropriate for each race. Our

An Alien Collective – Roxanne Barbour

abductors had given us a large supply of foodstuffs in our first supply drop.

After we picked up some food, the managing committee settled at a table to continue our planning. There was something I needed to discuss. "Stire, why was I pushed to the ground earlier?"

For a moment, Stire didn't answer. "Cyn, I am sorry about that. However, you must understand a little about Temmans. Physically, we're quite tall and strong. However, most of the time, if we lose our balance, we cannot recover and land on the ground. And, only slowly, can we regain our upright position."

"Yes, but why was I pushed?" I needed to know.

"Pushing is what we do to our enemies, and all aliens are, obviously, considered enemies."

"So, we're all at risk," said Jana.

"I'm afraid so. I will try and keep the Temmans under control, but don't count on it."

This is a fine state of affairs!

"Anything else I need to know about?" I glared around the table, but no one responded.

"What do we need to plan for tomorrow?" asked Stire; he needed to change the subject.

I noticed Frakis busy recording. "I've started a list," she said. "I just added 'find an escape' to it. It's all very well to follow the agenda of our abductors but I think…"

A loud screech erupted from everyone's universal translator. The sound was followed by a voice, saying, "Follow your instructions. Do not attempt to escape.

An Alien Collective – Roxanne Barbour

Any deviations from your agenda will be met with increasing repercussions." Then we heard a loud click resounding in the deathly quiet room.

This is not a good end to a very stressful day!

Gradually the dining area filled with conversation, but a note of hysteria was just below the surface.

"So it looks like our abductors read anything we record," said Jana.

"Yes," agreed Stire. "We must be careful. Let's continue our planning for now. We can discuss this later."

No one spoke for a moment, so I decided to bring up a non-controversial subject. "These chairs are certainly interesting. I don't know how they did it, but they seem to be comfortable for all of us."

"I agree," answered Stire. "Although we have some noticeable physical differences, they do work. Our abductors must have studied our planets for some significant length of time before they set up this village."

"And that's frightening," Frakis said. She was eating something that looked like canned purple worms. "I do have another subject I would like to bring up." She continued, "No insult to Stire, but this managing committee should be all female. That's the way we're organized on Reanno."

"Our abductors made it quite clear...."

Two humans burst through the cookhouse door carrying a third—someone who looked very sick. Jack and Hamza were toting Janet.

"Cyn, Janet just started throwing up a lot. What should we do?"

Chapter 3

Jack and Hamza gently deposited Janet on the floor of the cookhouse. I jumped up from my chair and ran over to her. Some of the others in the dining room moved as well.

Janet's face had a gray pallor and was shiny with sweat. She was conscious, but obviously in a great deal of discomfort.

"Has anyone found evidence of a hospital, or even medical equipment, in the village?" I asked in a raised voice.

A Temman spoke. "We may have found a medical clinic near where we woke up. It's a small building that contains some beds and equipment, although I may be forming incorrect conclusions about its purpose."

We need to get Jana there!

"Does anyone have any medical training?" I jumped when Stire spoke; I hadn't noticed him standing beside me.

A human and a Temman waved their hands.

Good. At least we have some medical expertise.

Stire pointed at the Temman. "Take us to the medical clinic quickly." He motioned for Jack and Hamza to pick up Janet and for the human and Temman medics to follow. Stire suggested to the remaining people in the cookhouse to turn in for the evening. It had been a long day, and we were all tired. He also suggested the managing committee proceed to the medical clinic. I needed no urging; I was not about to ignore a sick human.

The building was very close. We found a rudimentary medical clinic containing four beds, some examining equipment, and containers of drugs. The equipment and drugs were clearly segregated into four sections, and expertly labeled in our languages.

Stire, Frakis, and Jana went outside to join Jack and Hamza, so Janet could have a little privacy.

Lying on one of the beds, Janet looked so pale. She was still conscious, but her eyes wanted to close.

The two medics talked quietly to Janet while they examined her. I moved a little closer.

Janet looked up at me and said, "Sorry I'm such a bother. I don't know what happened. I started feeling tired after dinner, and then it got to the point where I could barely walk. So I sat down for a moment, and then I lost my dinner."

"Do you have any allergies?" one of the medics asked.

"Not that I know of. I probably just over-ate at dinner; every item I tried tasted so good." Janet had a little smile on her face.

An Alien Collective – Roxanne Barbour

"Did you try any of the alien foods?" I was curious about what had appealed to her.

"Just a couple; I do so love purple foods." Abruptly, Janet started to throw up again. A container was quickly found, and her discomfort was short lived. One of the medics gave her a glass of water to rinse her mouth and a damp cloth to wipe her face.

My eyes glanced at the bucket. Purple items did indeed make up the majority of the sludge. I gave the medics a *trust me* look before I spoke to Janet. "Believe it or not, Janet, I have an opinion. I think you have a case of food poisoning." The first part of my statement brought a smile to her face. "Your body is quickly getting rid of the offending items. You'll probably feel crappy for a few days, but if you just rest a lot, you should be better in no time." I gave her a pat, and then motioned the medics outside. "What do you think of my uneducated medical opinion?" I asked them.

"You're most likely correct. I was leaning towards that thought myself," answered a blond haired human. "But we should keep an eye on her, at least for tonight. Strik and I will split up the night watch. If all goes well, Janet could potentially rest in her own room tomorrow."

His name escaped me; then I remembered—it was Sam Jack. "Sam, I'm going to bunk here tonight too. Janet will be happy to have a familiar face."

"Sure, there's lots of room."

Together, the three of us walked back into the clinic.

"Janet, you lucky person, we've decided you're probably going to live. But guess what! You get to listen to my snores tonight." She relaxed a little. Our situation was not easy on anyone.

"Oh, good. I didn't want to stay here alone tonight."

"I'll be back shortly; I need to talk to the rest of the managing committee about tomorrow." I left Janet and paused on the steps of the medical clinic and took in the view. The setting sun infused the alien skyline with an unusual green hue.

I encountered Jack and Hamza hanging around the bottom of the stairs. "Thanks, guys, for bringing Janet so quickly. That was smart thinking," I said.

"We couldn't leave her on the ground; something was obviously wrong. So, we picked her up and took her to the only place where there could be some help. The medical clinic was unknown to us," said Jack.

"We haven't even been here a whole day yet. You couldn't have known." I was flabbergasted when I uttered those words. I had experienced so much in less than a day.

"What's the matter with her?" asked Hamza. He seemed a little agitated.

"Just a case of food poisoning from eating some alien food," I replied.

"Are you sure? Maybe she's infectious," he said. "Perhaps we should isolate her from everyone. Do you think she picked up an alien disease?" Hamza was wringing his hands.

Jack was behind him, so he could roll his eyes and not get caught. I stifled a laugh.

An Alien Collective – Roxanne Barbour

"Everything's fine, Hamza. Janet will rest here tonight, and I'm staying with her. Why don't you guys get a snack and have an early night. We all need a rest. And thanks again."

Jack put his arm around Hamza and gently hustled him away.

Stire, Jana, and Frakis were also waiting a few steps away. I went over to them.

"I'm going to stay here tonight; Janet needs a reassuring face. She should recover quickly. We think her experimentation with alien cuisine was too much for her system." I sighed. "I would have liked to try some alien foods, but it looks like I am going to abstain, at least for the time being."

A yawn escaped; I was so tired. "What do we need to plan for tomorrow?"

"Don't worry. We'll round up some cooks for the morning meal. If we have the meal at eight am; well, eight am by our timepieces, that is, we should get the cooks in around seven, or perhaps earlier. We'll let them decide. That should leave about nine hours for tonight's rest. Everything else can wait for tomorrow," answered Stire. He also looked weary.

"Sounds good. After breakfast, we'll need to go to Awakening Square and open the supply box. I'm a little apprehensive about what instructions we'll find," I said.

"We're all apprehensive, and we're all tired. See you in the morning," said Frakis with a weak smile.

So my first night was not spent in my new bedroom, but in the medical clinic.

An Alien Collective – Roxanne Barbour

During the late evening, Janet was only sick once. The medic on duty and I kept encouraging her to drink water, since dehydration would slow down her recovery. She didn't seem to need any pain medication, which was a relief for everyone.

Much to my surprise, Jana joined us around midnight. "What's up, Jana?" I asked.

"I was having trouble sleeping, so I decided to see if everything was alright here."

Jana is so sweet.

We chatted about inconsequential items for a while, and then Jana said, "You know, Cyn, this situation we're in is very troubling. We haven't a clue about how we got here; why we're here; what we're supposed to do...I could go on for quite a while. It's all very hard to grasp."

"I agree. And I imagine being surrounded by all these strange beings is unsettling for you. I know it is for me." Actually, I lied a little—I enjoyed interacting with aliens.

"I don't find it upsetting, but you all act very strangely at times."

We both laughed; Jana had uttered truth.

After a few moments, we joined in the slumbering.

In the morning, I woke up fairly well rested, and my shower only served to refresh me even more. However, we were going to have to do something about clothing.

"I need to get some new underwear. I'm wearing yesterday's," I said to Janet.

An Alien Collective – Roxanne Barbour

"I agree. At least they put some sanitary supplies in our backpacks."

Damn, I hadn't thought about that yet. Our abductors must have had an unimaginable set of details to juggle. "How are you feeling?" Janet had a little color in her face this morning.

"So much better! I may have to be a little less adventurous with the food, though."

"No argument from me." Medical crises were the last things we needed. "Do you want to go to breakfast?" She really didn't look rested, but I thought I would ask.

"No, I think I'll just stay here and sleep. I'm still feeling weak. Tonight, I might be brave and go to the cookhouse for dinner."

"I'll bring you some breakfast, but just a little bit," said Sam. He whistled a tune and set off.

I needed to get going. Today would be filled with unknowns. "Janet, I'll try to pop in later. The managing committee has so much to do today, so getting back here may be dicey. At the very least, I'll get someone to update you on the going-ons if you don't make it to dinner."

Because the time on my universal translator told me I was behind schedule, I rushed over to the cookhouse. I hastily threw some food on a plate and jumped into a seat at the table with the rest of the committee.

"How is Janet this morning?" asked Frakis.

"Much better, but she's very tired and is going to

An Alien Collective – Roxanne Barbour

rest all day. It looks like our diagnosis of food poisoning was correct. We'll have to be more careful to keep the food items separate." I so wanted to try some of the alien dishes. I sighed; a change of topic seemed desirable. "Frakis, what's the last memory you have before you woke up here?" I asked.

"Hmm. I had just finished dinner with my family, and I decided to take my *grasm* for a walk. My baby brother had been bugging me throughout the meal, and I wanted to get away from him. For a while, I watched Frik run around a little park, and then I woke up here." Frakis painted a vivid picture that could have been from a human home.

"What's a *grasm*?" I asked.

"A grasm is a small household pet. Frik has white fur, and is about two years old." Frakis's hand gestures gave me the image of a perky little dog. "I do miss my family," she added.

Stire interrupted, "Let's continue this discussion later. It's time to go."

And Stire was correct. The restlessness in the cookhouse was evident to all of us.

It didn't take long for Stire to gather up the crew in the cookhouse, and together we walked over to Awakening Square. After a moment's hesitation, the managing committee touched the supply box. To no one's surprise, it opened. Again, there were four sets of instructions.

"What do we have today?" someone yelled.

Stire gestured to the crowd for silence, and began to

An Alien Collective – Roxanne Barbour

read aloud. I followed along with my copy of the instructions.

"1. Another supply of wood has been delivered. You will need to search out your own source, as tomorrow will be the last day wood will be supplied. Cutting tools are included in today's shipment.

"2. Species specific seeds have been supplied. You will need to find the gardening tools and begin preparing gardens.

"3. All species can digest the animals found on this planet.

"4. Do not put items in the supply box."

Stire looked up. "No other instructions were included."

Item four had obviously resulted from yesterday's experiment with Frakis's scarf.

"Let's see what supplies they've given us today. We can discuss the instructions in a moment," suggested Frakis.

We unloaded the supply box and had the contents taken to the cookhouse. The cookhouse had evolved into our main meeting place.

We found more clothing, including three sets of underwear for everyone; at least, the alien equivalent of underwear.

Large and small cutting tools were in the shipment. We found seeds, of course, and food supplies. There was an additional supply of paper and some appropriate writing instruments, some heavy duty paper, tape, paints and brushes.

An Alien Collective – Roxanne Barbour

Do our abductors want us to stop using our recording devices?

While we were sorting everything out at the cookhouse, I commented, "We're being watched. How else would our abductors know I'd been talking about underwear?"

"If we're part of some alien experiment then it does make sense they want to watch what's going on," said Jana.

"Yes, but they must be watching everywhere. Yesterday, I was ranting loudly in my bedroom when I was changing into my new clothing. That must be where they heard me talking about underwear. It couldn't have been my conversation with Janet this morning; the supply box had probably already been filled by that time."

"That's most likely true," said Frakis.

"And I don't like it. But then, I don't like anything about this situation." I did manage a small smile. "Actually, that's not completely true. I'm happy we have absolutely confirmed aliens do exist."

Frakis laughed at my comment. "And how strange they look and act!" She did have a wicked sense of humor, at least in my opinion. And I was starting to lean towards the opinion that every species had a sense of humor—although I wasn't sure about the Irandi.

"Ok, let's decide what needs to be done," Frakis continued. "Our instructions involve some very big projects."

Stire broke in, "I agree with Frakis. We're going to have to be very careful how we allocate our resources;

there aren't many of us. We need to find a supply of wood, plant some gardens, hunt for a meat source, and, of course, continue the food preparation and cleanup."

They were daunting tasks but, with Frakis studying city planning, we had a tremendous resource on our side. Very quickly, the committee started to delegate tasks. Shortly, I noticed Hamza hovering behind me.

"Cyn, I don't want to be part of the search for wood. I want to be an explorer," said Hamza. "Let some aliens chop up firewood, and get hot and sweaty—or whatever it is they do."

Hamza is a thorn in my side.

I thought frantically. "Think of searching for wood as exploring the countryside. Who knows what you'll find?"

Hamza wasn't convinced. "I still think we should be able to choose whichever task we want."

"Don't worry; we'll be switching around the assignments."

Now go away and leave me alone.

When I didn't say any more, a sullen Hamza stomped off.

I guess grumbling wasn't relegated to just one species.

The managing committee decided to work with the gardening crew today. Appropriate tools had been discovered in the store room, so we gathered them up and went looking for our first garden patch. Since we would need a water supply, we looked for a spot near the creek.

An Alien Collective – Roxanne Barbour

A lovely open area near a small grove of trees was discovered. The grove would offer the workers a shady spot to rest when required. The gardening crew started by sitting under the trees and planning the layout of the garden.

Digging up the meadow made a long day for us but, thankfully, we had filled our packs with food and drink. Laboring in the garden area gave us ample time to think about our abductors and their threats.

By the time dinner drew near, I was exhausted. All I wanted was a shower and a nap. The nap wasn't going to happen but, after we returned to the village and put our tools away, I did take time for a shower.

One long wall of the bathroom was covered with a racking system. It dawned on me these were drying racks—a perfect place to hang newly washed clothes. I had changed into my new set of clothes, so I quickly washed my others. Our abductors had planned well.

Everyone seemed tired, so the atmosphere at dinner was subdued. The unreality of our situation was rapidly becoming very real. Our daily discussion began when most of us had finished eating.

Standing up and getting the attention of the room, I said, "Well I, for one, have run out of energy. Digging in the dirt will do that to you." Laughter rang out. "The good news is we have a small garden planted. More to come tomorrow." I got a round of applause, although I should be more accurate and say that the humans did the clapping, while the Temmans tapped on the table, and the Irandi and Reannone whistled. "Do we have a wood supply?" I asked.

A Reannone spoke up. "We have found a decent supply close by. The cutting tools were useful, and we have started a wood pile at the source. What we need to work on now is the best way to bring the wood back to our village. Since we're supposed to get another supply of wood tomorrow, we didn't bring any back today."

"Excellent," I replied. "Does anyone have any ideas on how to get the wood here, other than by armfuls, of course?"

"Actually, a group of us found some carts in a fenced area last night. They should work just fine for bringing back a load of wood," said Jack.

"Good going! I can tell you the gardeners were appreciative of the wheelbarrows found yesterday." I sat down, thinking that our situation seemed a little more optimistic today.

"Now, do we have any news on our meat supply? I could use some animal to chew on; other than any of you, of course." Jana's remark produced a sudden silence. Even though I had only known her for a little while, I decided she was trying to be funny, but the joke fell flat.

Strik, one of the medics, broke in quickly. "I was part of the hunting crew today. We did find one source of food: a herd of animals munching on the ground cover of an open field." He paused for a moment. "We did take some chances, though. One of us, slowly and carefully, walked up to one of the beasts and tied a rope around its neck. The animal wasn't alarmed, so we gave

An Alien Collective – Roxanne Barbour

the rope a tug, hoping the beast would follow. And it did. The animal was very placid. Our group had enough rope from the storeroom to bring back a little herd to a field adjacent to our village. We're hoping they'll stay there and not wander off."

"Well done! If they do start to stray, we can always put the herd in the pens we recently discovered. I think a nice activity after we've finished eating would be to take a stroll and look at these animals," Stire suggested.

Groups slowly formed and wandered outside.

Before I left for my stroll, I spoke with Janet. She had managed to take her dinner in the cookhouse. Although she was looking better, I agreed that lying down in her room would be about the extent of her physical exertion for the rest of the day.

The herd was placidly munching away where it had been left. Although the animals were about half the size of our normal beef cows, they were unlike any cow I had ever seen. They were uniformly black, with no markings of any kind on their hides. No tails were visible, and knobs adorned the top of their heads.

"What are we going to call these strange animals?" I asked.

"To me, they look somewhat like *graks*. *Graks* are a small herd animal on our planet," explained Frakis.

"Graks it is then. Does anyone know if we have any budding butchers in our group?"

"Actually, Temmans are taught to carve up animals," said Stire.

"Whatever for?"

An Alien Collective – Roxanne Barbour

Pushing and butchering, this is a little freaky!

"Historically, we are a nomadic race. In the past, because of the desert nature of our planet, we needed to wander in our search for water and food. That's not necessary anymore, because we have control of all water on our planet, but it's still in our nature to roam. Whenever we came across animals, we caught and butchered them. The tradition of learning how to butcher continues to this day." Stire moved his right hand in a circle. "Because roaming has been inbred, we actually move from city to city every two years."

"That must be annoying. You just get settled, and then you have to move again."

"Our years are about three times the length of yours, but it can still be annoying, as you say. However, there is a movement afoot right now that might change some of our rituals. We shall see."

I would have to think later about the ramifications of a nomadic life on an intelligent society. "Speaking of the length of the year, have we estimated the length of the days correctly?" I asked.

"It's about right. We may be a few minutes off, but it's nothing of any great significance. Let's leave our timepieces as they are," said Stire.

We watched the placid grak for a few moments.

"Perhaps it's time to go back. A good project for the rest of this evening might be getting everyone out to not just explore, but actually map our village. We could break up into four groups and apportion part of the village to each. We have lots of paper for mapping purposes; I'm just not sure how to do the measuring," said Frakis.

"Well, we could always count the number of footsteps," suggested Stire. "We just need someone in each group with approximately the same stride."

"Sounds logical," said Jana. "However, I have a couple of items I need to discuss, so I was hoping the managing committee could stay behind to hear me out."

What was bothering the Irandi?

After the others had left to map the village, we found out.

"The Irandi had a meeting before dinner—we had much to discuss," were Jana's first words. "I'm afraid this forced cooperation is bothering the Irandi. No clan is used to working with another clan. Generally, we work against each other. And working with aliens has most of us frightened. I'm just not sure how to handle the rest of the Irandi."

"Jana, you don't appear to be having a problem working with us," I commented as calmly as I could.

"That's not entirely true, but I can handle it because we're on a committee. We have a common goal, and a very serious one."

"How are your governments formed?" Before Jana had a chance to answer, Frakis interrupted. "Do you actually have governments?"

"We have various levels of managing bodies. They are formed by taking equal number from each of the six major clans."

"So your governments work well together?" asked Stire.

"For the most part."

"So, to be simplistic, we need to rename our work projects. If we call them committees, and make sure each committee has a representative from each race, do you think that'll work?"

Jana pondered that suggestion for a moment. "It might. It can't hurt to give it a try." She sighed and looked even more concerned. "The second problem the Irandi have is one of water."

Water?

"In our normal environment, we soak in warm water for about two hours a day. Our bodies need a moist environment for our health. I'm afraid the showers here are not good enough. We are starting to feel a little sick. We don't know what to do."

Chapter 4

I never expected this!
Needing a soak put a different slant on the Irandi.
"So let me get this straight: you need a big tub of warm water to soak in?"
Jana moved her head—in a nod, I assumed. "I know this is hard to understand, but our bodies are accustomed to it."
My mind tried to envision a horde of Irandi cavorting in a swimming pool.
"Does this pool of water have to be in a building, or can it be outside?" asked Stire.
"Preferably outside. Many generations ago, our ancestors built big ponds for soaking. So it's part of our culture, and our skin and internal organs seem to need the moisture."
"So what we need is a gigantic hot tub. That's what we call them on earth because humans also like to soak. All we need to do is dig a big hole in the ground, line the sides and bottoms with something—maybe wood,

find the source of our hot water, and somehow pipe it into the hot tub. Easy!" Everyone laughed at my humor. Nonetheless, the challenge seemed monumental to me.

"Can you last for another day?" Stire asked Jana.

"Yes, but in the meantime, we'll need to take some long showers."

"So this should be our priority project for tomorrow. It all sounds doable, but we'll need to get an early start. We have a lot of other tasks, and who knows what new instructions we'll receive in the morning." Taking control seemed natural for Stire.

Frakis was scribbling away on her universal translator.

"What are you doing?" I asked.

She smiled. "I'm a list maker, and always have been. I'm adding to my list everything we need to do tomorrow. Forgetting something might be a disaster."

"But I've noticed, Frakis, that you never forget anything," said Jana.

"Only because I make my lists." Frakis smiled and asked, "Jana, what's the last thing you remember before waking up here?"

"I don't remember anything." Jana looked away.

Jana didn't want to remember.

"Do you remember anything about that day? That might help you recover some thoughts."

Jana sighed, and gave in. "I remember having an argument with my mother over some cooking ritual. She's just so old fashioned. I was trying to convince her that some of her rituals were no longer used, but she wasn't having any of it. We were both quite annoyed. After dinner I went for a walk; I needed to clear my mind before I did some studying. That's the last I remember."

No wonder she had been reluctant to talk. I wouldn't want my most recent thoughts of my family to be an argument.

The mappers started to straggle back. We alerted them to tomorrow's major project. Our announcement created quite a buzz. For safe keeping, we gathered up the maps that had been made. Frakis added 'making a comprehensive map' to her own list.

After a little snacking, people started to wander off to their rooms.

In my room, I rested for a few moments before I decided it was time to start a journal. The solar lamp on the window ledge would help me see what I was recording.

Where shall I start?

I decided to start with my first waking thoughts in Awakening Square. After an hour or so, I got to the end of day one, and I decided that was fairly good progress.

With my eyelids drooping, I decided to call it a day. I took the turned-off solar lamp back to the window ledge, climbed in bed, and closed my eyes.

* * * *

Day three was again bright and cloudless. Would the weather ever change? Hopefully, our abductors would give us some notice. And, apparently, I had slept the sleep of the dead. Nary a dream was remembered.

An Alien Collective – Roxanne Barbour

As I chose my breakfast, I took a look at some of the other items on the countertop. There was an unusual pile of seeds, mostly a bright green color, which looked tasty. On the other hand, a couple of items look quite unattractive. I decided I wasn't brave enough to take the chance Janet had taken. Perhaps one day our captors would let us know our food compatibility.

The mood at breakfast was determined; we had a lot to accomplish today.

A commotion developed in the far corner of the eating area.

"I don't want to sit at the same table as any Irandi! They smell!" I strained to see who was ranting. A Reannone jumped up and stalked out the cookhouse door. I turned to Frakis and asked "Who was that?"

"That was one of our males, named Gree a Brewst. He's fifteen, and a bit of a hot-head, I'm finding. I've heard he studies marine biology at school, so you would think he would be used to various smells. He's just a little xenophobic; he's been trying to start arguments with everyone. I'll have a talk with him later today."

Jana stared at Frakis. "Do we smell?"

"You do have a slightly unusual smell—at least it's unusual to us, but we're all getting used to it. It's not unpleasant. Just ignore Gree." Both Frakis and Jana seemed a little embarrassed.

The mood on our walk over to Awakening Square after breakfast was subdued.

No instructions were found when we opened the supply box; just a lot of supplies. In fact, we received quite a few more supplies than we had on the previous day.

After everything was carted over to the cookhouse and put away, we rustled up a crew for the project of the day.

There had been a lot of buzz about why the *hot tub* was necessary. The other species were now viewing the Irandi in a new way. Until now, the general consensus had pegged the Irandi as fairly aloof.

The wood patrol from yesterday decided to stick together, and since it had members from all races, nothing needed to be changed. Although today's shipment of firewood was our last, their first priority was to make the liner for the hot tub. They would work on the wood pile a little later.

The six engineering students, who had been discovered in our group of thirty-two, discussed the shape and size of the hot tub with the renamed wood committee before it left to acquire the necessary lengths of tree trunks.

The engineering committee had decided it would be easier to maintain an in-ground hot tub, so the rest of us started to dig a big hole. The engineers escaped to find the source of the hot water and search out any other items that would be required for a simple hook up.

The hole for the soaker was being dug in an empty plot within viewing distance of the cookhouse.

Our big hole took most of the morning to dig. Upon the return of the engineers, we took a much needed break for lunch.

An Alien Collective – Roxanne Barbour

The engineering committee had been successful in finding the hot water source; it was a hot springs fairly close to the village. Apparently our abductors had piped hot and cold water into our facilities from the creek and the hot spring; and, much to the delight of the engineers, piping had been found at the back of the storeroom. For the time being, they were going to pipe the hot water from a nearby empty housing unit, but they were hoping to pipe it directly from the hot springs in the future.

Lunch time had been restful, but much more needed to be accomplished. The digging was finished, so a couple of the Temmans went off to butcher a grak. A small building adjacent to a fenced-in lot with running water would be converted to a butcher shop. The thought of roast grak on the dinner menu tonight made my mouth water. Let's hope I wasn't going to be disappointed.

Leaving the cooks and cleanup staff behind, the remaining few of us went back to being gardeners.

During our walk over to the garden, Frakis said to me, "I didn't see Gree a Brewst at lunch. I wonder where he could be."

"We'll have to send out a search party, I guess, if he's not back by dinner. I know he was upset at breakfast, but everyone needs to do their part for our alien collective," I said. "I hope it doesn't come down to some sort of disciplinary action."

Frakis looked concerned, but she didn't add anything to my comments.

The garden plot looked a lot smaller than what I

remembered. It seemed like we hadn't accomplished much yesterday, so we set steadily to work. A discussion on how to do successive planting ensued. The Temmans were not quite sure of the concept, as they were nomads, and the Reannone mostly ate everbearing water plants.

Frakis pointed at some seeds we had left boxed up. "We put some of these seeds aside yesterday because they look like our water plants. It would be nice to find some placid body of water to attempt to grow them."

"That brings up another subject: we're going to have to do some long range scouting soon," said Stire. "When we do, perhaps we'll find a lake, or something else suitable for your water plants."

"A lake would do. I suppose we could build a *cold tub*, as a last resort." Frakis smiled.

"Let's call it a *plant tub,* if it becomes necessary."

Tubs of water seem to be the current rage.

I continued, "Now that we've been here for a few days, what does everyone think about our situation? Any clues about why we're here? I know our abductors have told us not to try to escape, but shouldn't we at least think about it?"

"Escape where? How?" asked Jana.

"Oh, I have no idea. I'm just wondering how everyone feels about the situation, since we're getting into a bit of a routine."

"Well, as far as I am concerned, we're not meant to be here. The gods decide our fate at birth, and our life is all mapped out then," said Frakis.

"You have gods?"

"Yes. All our gods are female, although I never did figure out why. They decide our lives at birth, and our parents then let us know what our life work is going to be."

Did the parents get visions?

I decided not to ask about the details. It seemed pretty convenient for the parents, though.

Stire spoke up. "I don't know if it's possible to escape. We lack information. For example, we don't know where we are, or how we got here, or why we have been brought here. We need to study the situation carefully before any actions are taken. And we certainly shouldn't record anything."

Now that was a very conservative answer. I didn't know how creative the Temmans were going to be in finding an escape, but I did agree with not using the universal translator. Our abductors had made the situation perfectly clear when Frakis first recorded the word *escape*.

"We just have to accept our fate. We have been brought here for a reason, and we need to go along with the situation. Everything will work out in the end," said Jana.

"Well I, for one, want to escape. And I'm sure all the humans will agree. We do not take kindly to abduction and containment. So, I'm going to watch out for anything that will help us get out of here." I felt a little flushed after making those statements. There was no response from anyone.

An Alien Collective – Roxanne Barbour

And there we had it—four differing opinions.

During the afternoon, I learned a bit more about each of my roommates.

Stire spoke about his planet, Temma. Their dark mottled skin was for camouflage. Since, historically, they were nomads searching for water; their home became a warlike world as they fought over water sources. Temmans still instinctively want to move, and move they do. They leave their home to move to a different city for higher education; then every two long years after that they move to another city for employment.

"What is the structure of your family units?" asked Frakis.

"Not matriarchal, like yours," Stire answered. "Adults pretty much share all family responsibilities. Children become adults when they are six. All of us here are five years old, so we are close to becoming adults."

I still couldn't grasp the length of the Temman year. "Stire, what do you remember about the time before you woke up in Awakening Square?" I asked.

He thought for a moment. "I was going back to school after having my lunch at home. We live close to my pre-school."

"Sorry to interrupt, but what do you mean by pre-school?"

"This is the last school we attend before we move to another city for our higher education."

"Ah, I see. Please continue."

An Alien Collective – Roxanne Barbour

"There's a parkway along the route to school." He knew I would ask, so he added, "a parkway is a park with a walking path." Stire was looking, at least to me, a little melancholy. "Since I still had some time before class, I sat down on a bench to review some notes. Then I woke up here."

"I can't believe how similar our stories are," I said. I took a deep breath. "Across from my home is a small park. On a non-school day, when the weather was good, I would often take a textbook to the park and sit at a picnic table and do some homework. And that's the last I remember—studying some mathematics."

"I see what you mean," said Frakis. "We were all outside and by ourselves when we were abducted."

"Yes, and I'll never do that again," I said.

A little weak laughter escaped, but then silence surrounded us. We had a lot to think about.

As the day wore on, Jana spoke a few words about her culture. "We all belong to a clan but, unlike the Reannone, we have a great number of clans. Each clan distinguishes itself by the jewelry they wear on their fingers and arms." We all looked at Jana's hands. She did indeed have some fancy looking rings, but what I kept forgetting was the six fingers on each of her hands. It still awed me how elegant an upright lizard-like being could be. "Jana, are your clans distinguished from each other in other ways?" I asked.

"As you know, our first name is our clan name. Apart from that, most clans do tend to specialize in a trade. For example, there are clans who are experts in

An Alien Collective — Roxanne Barbour

machinery or administration. Our clan is a bit of an outcast because we like to explore. We're not entirely accepted because most of the Irandi are very conservative." She clapped her hands. "At least our current situation fits in with my clan."

We all laughed. Jana jumped a little when I gave her a pat on the back.

I asked, "Is yours a matriarchal society?"

"Ah no, not at all. Actually, we have what is called tri-archal relationships; two males and one female form a family bond."

That's unusual! Then I chided myself for being conservative; perhaps humans were the unusual species.

"But are there enough males to form these relationships?" Stire asked.

"Oh, yes. Twice as many males as females are born each year."

Is their society unique in inhabited space? For that matter, how much of space was inhabited?

For a while, we dug up more garden area. Then, Frakis looked like she wanted to say a few words. I wanted to pay careful attention; I found the idea of a matriarchal society quite different.

"Like the Irandi, we are clan-based, but our clans are based on the names of our four continents. For example, my name—Frakis a Kirba—means I am Frakis from the continent Kirba. The four continents are called Kirba, Camp, Simo, and Brewst. Reanno only has four continents; the rest of our surface is covered with water." Frakis thought for a moment, and then she said,

An Alien Collective – Roxanne Barbour

"We are a matriarchal society, and we always have been. I can't imagine anything else; that's why I'm having a hard time understanding the behavior of your societies. I'm going to try, though...What else can I tell you? Oh, yes. This large band around my head is actually an antenna. I know we also have ears, but the antenna lets us listen to other frequencies than normal. And when I say 'normal', I'm referring to the ones we all seem to hear. Actually, I'm quite surprised at how similar we are, in that respect. Oh, there are some physical differences, but our societies all seem to have family units, education, and work."

We planted seeds for a while until Stire said, "What can you tell us about your planet, Cyn?"

I knew my turn was going to eventually arrive.

What is important enough to mention? So I thought back to what the others had discussed.

"Our planet has a fair amount of water, but we have seven continents. In some respects, certainly in the past, our planet could be classified as warlike. Even now, we have the odd war, particularly in underdeveloped countries. In general, we don't have clans—although some would argue otherwise, but we certainly have rivalries. For example, each continent consists of numerous sovereign countries. Every two years, we have the Olympics—alternating between summer and winter. The Olympics are comprised of various seasonal athletic endeavors with competition between the countries. Our relationships, for the most part, are one female and one male, with no particular dominance." I told myself to

An Alien Collective – Roxanne Barbour

breathe. I had never thought about how we would appear to another alien race.

"Cyn, are you classified as an adult?" asked Stire.

"The definition of adult is different from country to country. For example, in one country the age for becoming an adult is eighteen. In another, the age is twenty-one. So, at seventeen, I am close to officially being an adult. But the number is just a legal convenience. I am physically able to have children. So, in my opinion, that makes me an adult. However I must add, although I am capable of having children, I don't necessarily think I'm mature enough to raise one."

We had all received a lot of information to digest, so we tabled our discussions and took our weary selves home.

Back at the village, there were some Irandi soaking in the newly finished hot tub. They were laughing and splashing. Thank goodness one crisis had been averted.

Dinner was a lively affair. The roast grak was the hit of the evening; it had a most unusual, but delicious, flavor. Thank goodness we now had a source of meat; it appeared to be a necessary item for all species.

"Does anyone know how the cooks are keeping our food refrigerated? Do we have any type of power supply?" I asked.

"I asked about refrigeration," said Jana. "There's some sort of in-ground container behind the cookhouse. Apparently, the creek water—which is quite cool—is piped around the container and keeps it cool enough for food to last a couple of days. Up until now, most of our

An Alien Collective – Roxanne Barbour

food has been canned or dried. Now that we have fresh meat, we have a way of preserving it for a short time. We'll also need this cooling facility when we start harvesting our greens."

"I wonder what else have our abductors have thought of, and we haven't yet discovered," said Frakis. It was a rhetorical question; we knew she didn't want an answer.

Just then, a male Reannone walked up to our table. "You wanted to see me, Frakis?" he asked.

"Yes, Gree. Where have you been all day?"

"Oh, I took a day off. I've been working too hard at these menial tasks. It was some alien's turn." Gree seemed quite defiant.

Frakis tapped the table. "It doesn't work that way, Gree. We all need to pull together and get our village running. We don't know why we're here, but we need to make the best of this situation. And making the best of it means everyone contributes. This is our life, for the time being. We're all taking turns at the tasks and, while I agree that most of them are menial, they're necessary for our survival."

"Well, I'm not going to do any." Gree straightened his posture.

Frakis glanced at us before she replied. "Then you don't get any food or housing. That's what we're all working for."

Gree stared at Frakis for a moment, and then walked away.

"Do you think he'll come around?" I asked her.

"Oh, yes. Our males are taught to obey females. Believe me, it makes it easier that a female Reannone is on our committee."

Yes, that would definitely work for a matriarchal society.

After dinner, more Irandi started soaking. I was standing outside, and it was obvious others were eyeing the hot tub. I turned to the other three. "Does anyone mind if people other than Irandi use the hot tub?"

"I don't see a problem. The engineering committee certainly designed a big enough one," Stire commented.

So we passed the word. Not everyone decided to soak, though. There were a few humans tossing some nicely rounded rocks back and forth, and a couple of Temmans were throwing sticks into a pile. Those activities niggled at my mind, and then it came to me. *Bocce ball!*

I knew Hamza was studying athletics, so I gestured him over. He needed to get over his fear of aliens. "Do you know how to play Bocce Ball?"

"Yes, I do. Why?"

"I think it's time to introduce everyone to Bocce Ball, and I'd like you to get it organized. Will you do that?"

"I guess so. We do need some organized social activities. I've been getting restless not having any."

It wasn't the most positive of responses, but it would do for a first step. "What about those round rocks you guys have been tossing about. Will those do? What else do you need?"

An Alien Collective – Roxanne Barbour

"I can always find something for a target, but we do need some way to color the rocks so they're different. Each player, or team, needs different colored balls…I mean rocks."

"Ah, you're in luck. We actually received some pots of paint and brushes today. They're probably for making signs or something, but they should work just fine for this project. I'll go get them for you while you get started."

Stire, Jana, and Frakis had listened while I talked to Hamza. They walked with me to the kitchen to fetch the paints.

"This seems to be an excellent activity you're planning," said Stire. "I don't know the rules, though."

"It's quite easy. We'll just have a little friendly competition. On Earth, at least, most people love games."

Hamza decided to paint four rocks red and four rocks green. He had found a strange looking rock for the target. A few beings had gathered around to see what the activity was all about. Thankfully, the paint was extremely quick drying.

"What we're going to try is a human game called Bocce Ball, but let's just call it *Ballz*. This strange looking item is called the target, but we're going to rename it the *Abductor*." A little anger was evident. "We'll randomly throw the Abductor for the first frame, but then the winner of the first frame will throw it for the next frame." Jack threw it out onto the grass of the empty plot where the hot tub was located.

An Alien Collective – Roxanne Barbour

"We'll need two teams of four players each. The players on one team will each get a red rock, and the other team will get green rocks. Then we're going to take turns throwing our rocks. After all rocks have been thrown, the rock closest to the Abductor gets a point for its team."

Hamza proceeded to throw four rocks. He threw one in a high arc; he rolled one down the grass; and a couple of them he threw right at the Abductor.

"You can see there are many ways of throwing your rock. I don't know if anyone noticed, but you can also hit the Abductor and move it away from an opposing team's rock so their rock is no longer the closest. Any questions?" Hamza was actually quite good at explanations.

Jana asked, "How is the game scored?"

"Good question; I forgot to mention anything about scoring. Once all of the rocks have been thrown, the judge goes to the Abductor and decides which rock is closest. A point is given to that rock's team. If two rocks from the same team are closest, the team gets two points. Then we do it again, meaning we do the next frame. When one team gets to thirteen points, the game is over, and they're the winner."

I looked around. There seemed to be some interested players. "Let's have mixed teams for our first try, one from each race," I said. "The managing committee would like to start, so who wants to make up the opposing team?" I hadn't asked Stire, Frakis, or Jana, but I heard no complaints.

An Alien Collective – Roxanne Barbour

"And I'll make up another set of rocks and Abductor so we can have a second game going on at the same time," said Hamza. He started looking through a pile of rocks to find more to paint.

The evening was quite enjoyable. The managing committee lost, but there was a lot of laughter. It turned out Stire had a competitive streak, and he just loved to move the Abductor. And Jana had the most accurate throw I had ever seen. We did indeed lose, but a little team spirit seemed to be forming.

I wanted to talk to the managing committee about something, so we stopped after playing one game. Back at the cookhouse, we had a little snack.

"What do you guys think about writing up some questions and putting them in the supply box? If we're going to survive, we need more information."

"I know the word you would probably use for my beliefs is fatalistic, but I don't think we're going to have a problem surviving. I'm sure our abductors have everything under control. And, don't forget, they told us not to put anything in the supply box," said Jana.

"Perhaps, but I think Cyn has an excellent idea. Even if they ignore us, they'll know we're trying to plan. I vote for her suggestion," said Stire.

"As do I," said Frakis. "We can never have enough information. Even receiving nothing from our abductors may tell us something."

I didn't quite know what Frakis meant, but I let it go for now.

Since our abductors had given us another batch of

An Alien Collective — Roxanne Barbour

paper and writing utensils, we gathered them up from where we had stored them in the cookhouse.

It took us a while, but we came up with a series of questions:
1. Why are we here?
2. How did we get here?
3. When will we be leaving?
4. Where are we?
5. What did we do to deserve this?
6. Will the weather change?
7. Will we always get supplies?

"There are probably many more questions we could ask, but we need the basics answered first," said Stire.

"Yes," agreed Frakis, "let's get these questions written up in each of our languages, and then put them in the supply box."

I looked forward to tomorrow's response.

Chapter 5

Only day four, but I would always remember it.

Breakfast time started off on an interesting note with a conversation with Janet. We went outside to have a private chat.

"Cyn, this is kind of a delicate matter." She hesitated, and then said, "I don't have any contraceptives with me. Is there any way we can get some?"

Birth control!

I decided to play this humorously. "Who's the lucky guy? I hope it's not Hamza."

"Actually, I have my eye on Jack. We've been having a lot of conversations lately, and actually spending a lot of time together. I really like him."

I can't believe this!

"Do you think it's wise to get involved with someone when we don't have a clue what's going on?"

"Probably not, but I'm so lonely. I miss all my family and friends back home. Actually, I miss my life." She looked a little misty-eyed. I did understand what she was feeling, and perhaps everyone in our village did too.

"Ok, what I'll do is send a note tonight to our abductors. Hopefully they'll respond. If not, we'll have to think of something else. Jack's a nice guy, but just be very careful."

"Oh, I'll be careful. So what about *your* secret admirer?"

"What are you talking about? I don't have an admirer." I was confused.

"That's why I said *secret admirer*. There is definitely someone keeping an eye on you, but you'll have to find out for yourself."

"You're so dead!" I said. Janet just grinned and walked away.

I was going to kill her for teasing me like that. Now I was going to be looking over my shoulder all the time.

My journal needed to be updated this evening. There was so much going on.

* * * *

Back at the breakfast table, where the rest of the committee was finishing up their first meal of the day, Jana asked, "What was that all about, Cyn?"

"It's a little hard to explain. Actually, the subject can sometimes be taboo for humans."

Frakis said, "That's easy. It's about sex, isn't it?"

I nodded.

"What kind of problem is Janet having? Surely some human male is available for her?"

I choked and spluttered. I decided not to explain

An Alien Collective – Roxanne Barbour

human relationships. It was not the time, especially since I didn't understand a lot myself. "Well, she has her eye on someone, but she wants to be careful if the time comes for intercourse."

"Why does she have to be careful? Will she be hurt?"

"No, no, not at all. She just doesn't want to have a baby, particularly in our situation. So she's asked me to get some contraceptives."

"What are contraceptives?" asked Frakis.

"They prevent a female from becoming pregnant."

"So you don't naturally control conception?" asked Stire.

"No, that's not possible for humans. Every physical interaction doesn't necessarily produce a baby. In fact, it can sometimes be very difficult to become pregnant. Contraceptives give women control, so they can choose the time to have a child."

"Female Temmans can naturally control conception, so we don't have a problem like you humans do," said Stire. That sounded a little smug to me.

"What about the Irandi?" Stire asked Jana.

"We have no natural control, either. However, we believe that if conception happens, it was meant to be. Contraceptives have never been part of our culture because conception can be very difficult. So our relationships have evolved into two males and a female; to double the chances of conception."

Double the fun!

With what I thought was amusement showing on

the faces of Stire and Jana, we all looked at Frakis.

"We have a little bit of everything. We can physically control conception, to a certain degree. However, I am not going to discuss that because it is something of a taboo; however, we also use contraceptives. So on our list tonight to our abductors we should also include a request for contraceptives for the Humans and the Reannone."

I am astounded by the differences between us!

Before we divvied up the personnel for our work crews, we went to Awakening Square. Everything looked so calm and peaceful, and the sky was again clear. *Will I ever feel rain again, or even see clouds?*

The managing committee was full of anticipation. What answers would we get to our questions?

However, we were greatly disappointed. There were no new instructions in the supply box, and no answers to last night's questions. The sheets of paper with the questions had disappeared, though. The supply box was full, and we had a new item; some rolls of very strong looking wire had appeared.

All the supplies were taken back to the cookhouse and stowed away. We didn't know what the rolls of wire were for, so they were put in the store room for the time being.

Duties were reassigned, and some new ones added. A small lake had been discovered nearby, so a couple of people were going to try some fishing.

Gree was behaving himself today. He uttered no complaints when he was put on the wood chopping detail.

An Alien Collective – Roxanne Barbour

The managing committee decided it was time to take a scouting trip. We needed to see more of the countryside. Some long range planning was necessary, and we wanted to search out a source of fruit—if there was any to be had.

Since we were all needed to open the supply box each morning, a day trip was the only thing possible for the committee.

Our packs were filled with food and water for the day. Everyone seemed to be in excellent shape, so we set off at a brisk pace.

Around the village, slightly rolling fields were most evident. However, in the distance, we could see a stand of trees. So we headed north-west, or at least the direction we had designated north-west. The stand of trees was our best chance for finding fruit.

Passing through the fields, small animals scurried away from us. They looked like small brown chickens, more or less.

"Those animals must be edible, according to our new notes from our abductors," I said.

"We would have to catch a lot to feed everyone. And I don't know how easily they could be caught; they look to be quite quick," replied Stire.

"Something to add to Frakis's list. Perhaps someone is a natural hunter, and could come up with a viable plan."

I continued, "There are a lot of flowers in these fields. I wonder if they're edible. We love having flowers on our salads."

An Alien Collective – Roxanne Barbour

"One of the words you just said did not translate," said Jana. "It was the word where you said you put edible flowers on your *something*?"

"Oh, you mean salad. Think of it as raw vegetables. We like having a bowl of raw vegetables—of many different varieties—with a sauce on top; that's what we call a salad." This time I could hear the word salad, so it was now available to everyone. Apparently, our universal translator had some intelligence and could update itself.

"That's an interesting concept," said Frakis. "In general, most of our food is cooked. I'll have to try some of our food raw when we get some produce from the gardens."

The stand of trees that we were aiming for was on our side of the creek, so that made our trip a little easier.

My neck was becoming a little sore from my head swiveling around to keep everything in sight; I didn't want to miss any small detail.

Something seems to be missing.

"Has anyone seen any birds?" I asked. It seemed strange not to see objects flying in the sky. At home, the birds were always flocking around our feeder.

The committee seemed to know what I was talking about, so there hadn't been another universal translator miscommunication.

"No, not a single bird," answered Frakis. "That is indeed unusual."

At the edge of the forest, there were a couple of slight mounds of earth with some large smooth rocks on top. A food break and a short rest were in order.

"Cyn, I did like the game we played last night—even though we didn't win. It was straightforward, yet very strategic. Do you have any other games like Ballz?" asked Jana.

So Jana is a game player!

"Oh, I'm sure we can come up with something; humans do play a lot of games. How about the rest of you? Do you know of any games that would be suitable for our group? Like card games, or maybe athletic games?"

That question bounced around our heads for a moment or two.

Since no one spoke, I said, "Let's create an entertainment committee this evening. It's important to keep busy, so we don't have time to think about our predicament." I sighed. "Other than family and friends, there is one thing that I'm missing a great deal. I need my daily fix of books to read."

"What kind of books do you read?" Stire asked.

"Oh, mostly fiction. I love my mysteries, and the stories about aliens." I had to laugh; I was living one of my novels.

"I also read a lot. Although I do read the occasional book of fiction, my reading is mostly technical books; books on chemistry and the search and preservation of water," continued Stire.

Since neither Frakis nor Jana seemed to have a comment about reading, we packed up and entered the forest.

An Alien Collective – Roxanne Barbour

The forest consisted of small patches of trees interspersed with tiny meadows. The sunlight shining into the meadows created some pleasant areas. The trees were quite small and somewhat oddly shaped, but certainly recognizable as trees. Again, no birds were seen or heard.

Happily, quite a few of the trees had fruit. The next couple of hours were spent cataloguing the fruit, and putting samples in our packs.

We found some blue fruit the size of apples, and a yellow fruit that looked like a small melon. A few of the trees were sparse with fruit, but we did find a loaded tree that had something similar looking to green plums. The ground beneath that tree was covered in rotting fruit.

Some unfamiliar sounds were heard in the trees while we were collecting our samples. They sounded like quiet shrieks. I was a little uneasy. Obviously there was an animal up in the canopy.

Then we discovered a tree with fruit that looked familiar to me.

"Those look like coconuts," I said.

"And to me, those are similar to *teera*. I'm going to climb up to take a look," said Jana. "Stire, could you give me a lift please? I'll throw some of the fruit down when I get high enough.-I hope they're similar to our fruit; teera are so delicious."

It took a couple of minutes for Jana to climb high enough. Then the teera started to rain down.

We quickly picked them up, and then backed away.

The size and weight of the teera would have raised a considerable bump if we had been in the wrong place.

Jana called out, "Guys, I see something in the leaves. It's coming towards me; I'm retreating."

Just then another teera fell, and we heard a scream.

The next thing we knew, Jana landed at our feet. She was in terrible shape. One of her arms had been broken, and she was bleeding in numerous spots. She was unconscious, but still breathing. I had a towel in my pack, so we tore that up and used it to stop her bleeding. We were mostly successful.

"We need to get her back to the village—to the medics and to her own people," said Stire. "I am able to carry her, but I need someone to take my pack."

Not a sound was heard in the forest as we arranged our packs.

We stopped a couple of times on the way back to give Stire a rest. We weren't in the mood for much conversation, either, although Stire did say, at one point, "We have been taking our surroundings too much for granted. This is not necessarily a benign world."

At our third stop, Stire carefully placed Jana on the ground. "She has turned cold. I think Jana has died."

Chapter 6

I can't believe this! Not Jana! Stire has to be wrong!

Jana's chest was very still, and she didn't appear to be breathing. I bent over and tried to find her pulse. I couldn't, but perhaps I was touching the wrong spot for an Irandi.

"You may be right, Stire. Jana has certainly lost some blood. Let's get her back to her own people; I'm sure an Irandi will be able to tell better than we can."

I couldn't think clearly. My mind was racing, and my nerves were twitching.

We continued our journey back, and a very quiet journey it was. Even the sun seemed a little less bright. We weren't dawdling, but the trip seemed to take forever.

At the village, it was close to dinner time. As soon as we arrived, the word spread and everyone quickly gathered together. The Irandi hovered around Jana.

A very tall Irandi approached us and gave Stire a

push. "What have you done to Jana?" Then he turned to Frakis and me and said, "Who did this to Jana?"

My voice cracked as I said, "Nobody did this to Jana. She fell out of a tree!"

The Irandi took a step back.

Frakis interjected, "Are there any Irandi with medical knowledge?"

The one Irandi with some medical experience made an examination. "Jana is indeed dead. She has lost too much blood. You did a good job in stopping the bleeding, but we Irandi cannot suffer much loss of blood. That, along with the broken bones, caused her death."

"Whatever animal attacked her is the real culprit. But we'll discuss that later." My hands didn't know what to do with themselves. I needed to calm down. Our abductors hadn't appeared, so we going to have to deal with this ourselves. I took a deep breath, and continued, "What kind of death rituals do the Irandi have?" Death was such a harsh word. "What needs to be done now?"

Gola Cho, the male Irandi who had examined Jana, spoke up. "We need to clean Jana up, and then she needs to lie on display for two days. This is our mourning period when everyone has their chance to pay their last respects. We do a lot of talking to a recently deceased person. After two days, we have a ceremony."

"Do you need a secluded place for this ritual?"

Cho motioned affirmation.

"How about one of those empty buildings on the edge of the village?" asked Stire. He pointed north.

"That should do just fine." Although we heard a lot of grumbling, Cho quickly organized the other Irandi, and they carried Jana away.

I was suddenly feeling very sad and tired; the stress of our whole situation was catching up with me. I wanted to go home. Loneliness was not what it was cracked up to be.

* * * *

Dinner was quite a somber affair.

Our normal food items had been supplemented by a couple of fish dishes. The fish were odd looking. They had an almost rectangular shape, and the colors were very dark. However, the taste was exquisite; the cooks had fried them in a kind of sweet sauce. My fish was supplemented with some of the tasty grak.

Most of the chatter I heard was about the food and, of course, Jana's death.

As the end of dinner neared, I said to Stire and Frakis, "We need to keep people occupied. I suggest we create our entertainment committee now, and then get everyone outside. We'll keep them engaged in some activity—even if it's only soaking in the tub."

"Agreed," said Stire. Frakis just nodded.

"I'll say a few words," Stire added.

Stire stood up and got everyone's attention. "As I am sure everyone knows, Jana had an unfortunate accident today. We will be taking measures to make sure this doesn't happen again. A ceremony honoring her life will take place after two days of visitation. It is Irandi custom to spend some time with the deceased before the ceremony. The Irandi will, of course, be spending time with Jana. If anyone else wishes to do this, I have been assured the Irandi would be honored.

"On a brighter note, we did find a supply of fruit. And I can see that everyone enjoyed their fresh fish. Frakis, Cyn, and I have some issues to discuss right now, but the first item we want to share is the formation of an Entertainment Committee. The Ballz game was enjoyed by many yesterday, so we want a committee to come up with other games and activities. If anyone is interested in being a member of the entertainment committee, please let us know. We're going to keep the committee small, just one from each race. In the meantime, go out and soak, or play some Ballz." Stire sat down again at our table.

"Nice speech," commented Frakis. "It was right to the point. I mean, you covered all the topics that were important."

"Thanks. I didn't want to belabor Jana's death, and I wanted to get everyone active and occupied again. Now, the three of us have some important decisions to make."

Before we could start our discussion, people started arriving at our table—eager participants for the entertainment committee. The first person from each race was chosen, and then sent them off to be inspired. After we cleaned off our table, we set to work.

"I think our most important issue is the supply box," said Stire. "Up until now, it has required the four of us. Now that Jana is dead, what's going to happen?"

An Alien Collective – Roxanne Barbour

"I don't know. Perhaps the supply box will open with just the three of us. As you know, I do believe our abductors are watching us, so they should know what's happened. It's likely that they will alter the box, but if they don't, what can we do?" I asked.

"I think we should make up a list again, and put it in the supply box tonight. One of the items on the list could be a question about what happens with the managing committee now that one of us has died. Our abductors may not have even thought about this possibility."

Frakis's response was interesting.

"You might be right about that; although they seem to have thought of everything else," commented Stire. "So let's put in a note about Jana, but I also think we should choose an Irandi to approach the supply box with us tomorrow morning—just in case all we need is Irandi DNA."

After a little more discussion, that plan was agreed upon.

"I was also thinking about the fruit we found today. Realistically, we should ask our abductors if we can eat the fruit without being poisoned, and also about the compatibility of our own foods. We don't want any more incidents like the one involving Janet. And what do we know about the wildlife? Apparently, we have found one hostile life form already. How many more are there? If we want to harvest the fruit, we may need weapons of some sort. I think we should explain that in our notes. Let's start calling them 'reverse instructions'. It's time we gave our captors a poke." I was in the mood for a confrontation.

An Alien Collective – Roxanne Barbour

"Good," said Frakis. "I also think we should include our questions from yesterday. However, let's add an instruction:'please answer the following questions:' Let's see what that will get us. If we upset them enough, maybe they'll let us go."

I didn't think Frakis really expected that to happen. The death of Jana must have put her on edge.

"And I do need to have the question of contraceptives raised," I added.

So we found our writing supplies and wrote up our *instructions and questions* in three languages. Once the notes were deposited in the supply box, we headed back to the *gaming area*. It amazed me how quickly objects got names that stuck.

There were a couple of games of Ballz going on, but something else was happening. A pile of empty food tins was visible, and a flat piece of wood, about six by six feet, was having some holes drilled in it. The flat piece of wood was sitting on four chunks of logs that were lifting it off the ground. The food tins were being painted yellow and blue.

"I think we should make the holes about two times the size of the can bottoms," said Brik, a Camp. "That's a bit bigger than in the game of *Campene*. We need to give the competitors a chance, because we don't have soft balls to use. Soft balls are more flexible and slide through the holes more easily." The Irandi holding the wood cutting tool started to widen the hole.

"What's this all about?" asked Frakis.

Brik replied, "We have designed a new game. It is

An Alien Collective – Roxanne Barbour

based on Campene." Frakis nodded her understanding. Brik looked at Stire and me and said, "You have two teams with their colored cans. You throw the can towards one of the four holes in the wood. If it lands and stays on the wood, it is worth one point. If it goes through a hole, it is worth three points. And to put some offensive strategy in, you can always knock an opponent's can off. Pretty simple game; in some respects similar to Ballz. Again, we're going with thirteen points to win. The equipment may need a little adjustment; we'll try some games and see how it goes."

"Good work," said Stire. "I want to try this game; it seems familiar. We may have a children's game at home similar to it, but I'm not sure. Games haven't been a big part of my life."

"Give us ten minutes," said Brik. "The paint needs to dry a bit. In the meantime, we're going to try and make up a name for it."

We wandered over to the Ballz games. Interestingly, all of the teams seemed to be mixed—one from each race. I walked up to Strik, who apparently was today's organizer. "How did you manage to get all of these teams to be mixed?"

"That was easy. I announced that we would be having a two day tournament; it would be one house against the other. By the way, we painted numbers on the housing units today. We numbered yours *one*." We all laughed, and Strik continued, "Tonight's the practice night, so the housing teams are practicing. There seems to be quite a competitive streak developing."

An Alien Collective – Roxanne Barbour

"How is our house going to be able to compete?" Frakis asked.

Strik replied, "Since I'm the judge for the tournament, I will make up a rule that says you can borrow an Irandi whenever necessary. Obviously not when you are playing the team that the Irandi is from, but we'll make it work."

"Good; my competitive gene was twitching. The tournament sounds like fun," I said.

Stire gave me a strange look. Perhaps the image of a twitching gene bothered him. I knew he would let me know what he was thinking, eventually.

I needed a camera to start recording memories.

My thoughts turned to Jana. Over the last couple of days, I felt that I had started to become friends with Jana; her input in our discussions was going to be missed. I would have to go and sit with her for a while tomorrow.

"I think it's time to try out that new game," I suggested to Stire and Frakis.

There were a few people throwing cans when we arrived at the playing area.

"Time for a game of *Spider*?" Brik asked us.

"Spider is an unusual name," said Frakis. "How did you come up with that?"

"Oh, Jack thought the cans falling off the edge looked like spiders plopping down, and I thought of a similar Reannone insect, so the name stuck."

Brik joined the three of us as a team, and we started to get slaughtered. Apparently, none of us had much of an aim. One of the main problems was that the cans rolled off the wood too easily.

"Brik, these cans just don't make it. We need something like bean bags—bags that have seeds or little stones, or something like that, in them—that way they'll stay on the playing surface," I said.

"You're right. And you've made me think of the perfect way to create them. When I was fishing, I saw a pebbly beach at the lake. We can gather some of the smaller ones tomorrow and put them in bags. There must be some cloth somewhere; maybe we can use our old clothing. And the medical clinic must have needles and thread."

"That should be a great improvement; this was a good start, though. I'm looking forward to your next innovations," said Stire. "I don't know about the rest of you, but I think I need an early night, with some clothes washing thrown in. Cyn, will you join me?"

"Yes, I'm quite tired. It's been a stressful day."

Frakis waved at us as she went over to the Ballz games.

Stire and I slowly walked over to housing unit number one.

I decided Strik must have a sense of humor; or maybe he was just being logical. I decided to stick with the sense of humor. Seeing the number one on our housing unit made me smile once again.

Stire and I sat down on the couch in our living area.

"Since we each received an additional set of clothing this morning, I think I'm going to pass on the washing," I said.

"I believe I am too tired to do any cleaning, as well. Let's just sit here and chat for a while. We don't seem to get much personal time; our days are so busy being on the managing committee."

That seemed an odd thing for Stire to say, but I didn't have the energy to move.

"Cyn, do you have a male friend back home? I mean someone to whom you are attracted?"

"Not really. I certainly have male friends, but nothing serious. We're just friends; we spend time together engaging in various cultural and social activities."

Why is Stire asking this? Perhaps he was curious about our society.

It was my turn. "What about you, Stire?"

"I have no serious female friend at this time. Recently, I've been spending most of my time on my studies. There is so much to do and learn at my age."

"I know what you mean. I'm trying to study mathematics and computer science; they are such vast subjects. You know, this situation of ours is so bizarre. I should be at school learning all sorts of new things." I started to feel depressed.

"Cyn, cheer up. Yes, this is a difficult situation, but you're handling it so well. I'm very impressed with your ability to cope with such major change. I am quite pleased that you were selected for the managing committee; it has made my life a lot easier." Stire put his arm around my shoulders, and gathered me in.

What is happening?

Chapter 7

Stire had quite a sweet scent, and it was comforting to be held.

Frakis arrived shortly and said, "All right you guys, no sleeping in our common area." And she shooed us off to our own rooms.

And I had fallen asleep!

I got ready for bed in a tired blur. As I closed my eyes, I suddenly remembered Stire putting his arm around me. *Oh my!* The result was an unusually restless night. I spent a lot of time thinking about Stire; I came to no conclusions about my feelings.

The next morning, the mood at our breakfast table was fairly subdued. Jana's empty place lent a somber tone to the atmosphere.

"I wonder what delights await us this morning," said Frakis. "I hope some of our questions have been answered."

"Surely they will be. This is the second time we've asked most of them. They must realize we're anxious.

An Alien Collective – Roxanne Barbour

It's not like our abductors will lose some control by giving out a couple of tidbits. This operation is so well planned that they've even provided us with solar lights, so a power supply was not required. How controlling is that?" I felt like I babbled. Perhaps Stire made me a little nervous.

The path to Awakening Square was starting to show a little wear. It had originally been covered in tiny stones, but now ruts began to show. One cause of the ruts was the walking we did with the supplies each morning. Perhaps a still greater cause was the carts now being used to haul the daily wood. Each cart needed two people to pull it, but they could carry a great deal more wood than anything else we had.

Everyone was more than a little anxious when we approached the supply box for the first time after Jana's death. Gola Cho was standing by.

However, the supply box opened easily without Irandi DNA.

We were disappointed when we looked inside. There were no written answers to our questions, but that wasn't entirely correct. There was a note that said the fruit was safe to eat, and that we were being supplied with new packs for everyone to use whenever we left the village; the old packs were only to be used as storage. But our burning questions still had no answers.

A couple of new items were the requested contraceptives and some big rolls of metal fencing—at least it looked like the rolls could serve as fencing.

"I don't see any weapons," said Frakis. "Since

we've been told the fruit is harmless, you would think they would give us something with which to defend ourselves."

"Maybe that's what they are implying by the fencing—to keep us safe while we are in the village. Or maybe it's just for our herd of grak," Stire added.

"I wonder if there's enough fencing to do both." I definitely didn't want our source of meat to be attacked.

"Let's leave the fencing here for a moment and take the rest of the supplies back to the cookhouse," Stire said to the crowd.

On our way back, I saw Frakis looking at a pile of stones in a corner of Awakening Square.

"What are those?" I asked her.

"A couple of Reannone collected stones from the lakeshore. They built a shrine to our gods, so we could do a little peaceful meditation."

"That's interesting. We're starting to make our village a home."

Frakis only smiled.

Back at the cookhouse, we had our regular discussion after the day's delivery had been stored.

In the end, two major work parties were assigned. One work party would begin fencing the village and the graks, and the other one would attempt to make some weapons. We needed some protection, especially when collecting fruit. The weapons committee hoped there would be some suitable supplies in the storeroom. If nothing else, they were going to make some spears; the wood cutting equipment would help sharpen them.

An Alien Collective – Roxanne Barbour

The managing committee decided to investigate the path we had discovered on our first day.

In the end, only Stire and I took off on the trek; Frakis decided to stay behind and help with the gardening.

"I'm in need of some spiritual healing. Being close to the earth will help."

Shortly, Stire and I loaded up our new packs and took off.

"Why do you think we were given these new packs?" I asked.

"There could be numerous reasons. The packs could be stronger; they could be water resistant; they could have a homing device. I don't know. Our abductors are obviously *alien* in their thinking, so we may never guess the right answer." I hoped that was another example of Temman humor.

We didn't talk a lot as we walked west. In Stire's presence, I felt a little uncomfortable. Neither of us broached the subject of last evening's cuddle.

We first passed through a small grove of trees and emerged into a meadow-like area. At this point, the path was quite wide, in good shape, and lined with small stones.

The path sloped slightly downhill. In the distance, another grove of trees came into view. At the center of the grove there was a large, open area. Our path was leading us directly there. After about an hour, we reached the edge of the trees.

"Let's have a little rest and a snack," I suggested. "I

An Alien Collective – Roxanne Barbour

don't think I ate enough at breakfast; I'm starving." My arrival on this planet hadn't changed my appetite.

While we ate, I looked around. In the distance, our village appeared at a slightly higher elevation; our home looked so peaceful in the sunlight. Behind the village, some mountains rose into view. Only a small amount of snow was visible on the mountain peaks. Perhaps our corner of this planet had a very temperate climate.

This forest appeared similar to the grove of fruit trees we had previously found.

"Let's get through quickly," said Stire. "It reminds me of where Jana died. I don't want to run into any animals." We were both fleet of foot, so we started running.

Shortly we burst out of the forest and came to an abrupt halt in a large cleared area. Unbelievably, a small ancient village appeared before our eyes. The tumbled ruins were covered with vines and other vegetation.

"Look at those ruins," I said, grinning from ear to ear. "They're obviously very ancient, because the stones look smooth and weathered. Do you think our abductors put in the path so we could find this?"

Stire looked a little skeptical. "Perhaps. Why don't we climb up to that high point? We can probably see the entire site from there."

I looked where he was pointing. It did look like the high point, and I wanted a clear view of our surroundings.

The climbing was a bit arduous; the stones were

very smooth. Some vines helped our climb, but it was still very treacherous.

At the top, I plunked myself down. Stire and I spent a couple of minutes not saying a word. We needed to recover some energy.

Stire interrupted our silence. "Cyn, I need to talk to you about something now that we're alone."

Oh, no! I don't think so.

"Ah, not right now. I want to study this; I love being an explorer."

Not on your life, Stire. I was too confused to deal with him at the moment.

"Ok, we'll have our discussion later."

I didn't know how to interpret the look on his alien face. Ignoring the whole subject, I turned back to studying the area.

The village appeared to have been built in a circle; the highest spot was where we were sitting. That was pure conjecture, though, since we didn't know what the village looked like before its abandonment.

"It looks like the roads of this village converged just down below us," said Stire.

"Perhaps this was the main square. Let's explore for a couple of hours, and then return home."

Stire paused for a moment. "You know, we should have a name for our own village. It seems strange just calling it 'the village'. And this one should have a name too. In fact, we should start some long range mapping."

"You're right. Maybe we should have a contest to name the villages and other areas."

An Alien Collective – Roxanne Barbour

"Excellent idea! And a prize would be appropriate!" We were both in a better mood after that discussion.

Carefully, we climbed down and wandered around together. The majority of the buildings were just piles of stone. The odd time we found a wall intact, we could see that the previous inhabitants liked the round shape. In addition to the village, the doorways and windows were also rounded.

Unfortunately, we didn't find any artifacts in our meanderings. The village appeared to have been abandoned a very long time ago, so perhaps the inhabitants cleaned out the village when they left.

Something caught my eye.

"Stire, there's another tall ruined structure up ahead. I'm going to do some climbing and see if I can get a better view. I might find a building that looks promising."

Stire just nodded. He hadn't said much lately.

I found a few climbable vines. On my way up, I noticed considerably more dust and grit than we had previously experienced. As a result, the climb was more difficult. Part way up, I turned around to look at the city below.

The vine that I was clutching came loose from the stones.

The next thing I knew, Stire was giving me a little shake. I was lying on the ground, and, oh, did I ache!

"What happened?" My thoughts were clearly jumbled.

"You decided to fall down to get my attention. Really, Cyn, I have been paying attention to you."

An Alien Collective – Roxanne Barbour

I hoped Stire was trying to be funny. Sitting up hurt a little, but it was doable. I just sat and breathed for a few moments.

"How do you feel? You don't appear to be bleeding very much. I only see a few scratches."

Stire is very anxious.

"I feel like I've been run over by a large vehicle. My whole body aches, and I have a wicked headache."

"I think you may have a concussion. You were unconscious for a couple of minutes. Can you stand?"

"Oh, sure, just help me up."

Stire lifted me up. I started to collapse, but he caught me.

"I can't stand on my ankle. I think it must be broken." The pain brought tears to my eyes. "You need to go home and get a cart and a couple of other able bodies. Then you can cart me back to the village."

Stire studied me.

What the hell is he thinking?

"No, I can carry you. You're even smaller than Jana, so you shouldn't be a problem."

This was not an argument I was going to win; Stire seemed determined. Staying here by myself wasn't an option I wanted to face, anyway.

We organized our packs. At this point, they weighed very little. Stire lifted me up. It was slow going until we reached the path, and then our walking rhythm settled down.

The last thing I remember is Stire saying, "At last I have you in my arms."

Chapter 8

A sneeze woke me up. I discovered I was lying on a bed in the medical clinic. When I looked up, I realized that Stire, Cho, and Sam hovered over me.

"Nice sneeze! How are you feeling?" asked Sam. "You should have a headache, just in case you're wondering." I decided Sam would make a great doctor.

My body parts took exception to my wriggling about, but I was determined to sit up. "I definitely have a headache, and my ankle is killing me. Is it broken? I sure hope not; I have a lot of things to do." The pain was making me ramble.

"No, your ankle's not broken; just badly sprained. But, realistically, you're not going to be doing much more than sitting around for at least a few days. Amongst the bottles of pills, I found one labeled 'Human: for Pain/Swelling.' So, I think this bottle is for you." Sam handed me a small bottle of red pills. "Just start with one pill. We don't know how strong they are, or how they may affect you."

An Alien Collective – Roxanne Barbour

I watched Sam turn away from us. After he turned back, he said, "Also I want you to keep your foot elevated and cool."

"Cool? How am I going to do that?"

"Soak your ankle in the creek a couple of times a day. The water is quite cool. And here, try these crutches."

He handed me an interesting pair of crutches. They had numerous sliding adjustments, and appeared to be made of plastic. It looked like they could be modified for any race. I slid off the bed and leaned against it. Cho helped me adjust the crutches for my height.

"Hobble over to the sink and take one of your pills." My immediate thought was that Sam wanted to see if I could handle the crutches.

"Are you up to this, Cyn?" asked Stire.

"Oh, I think so. I can't sit in this bed all day." I lurched over to the sink and got a glass of water. My strength had pretty much disappeared, but I wasn't going to let them know that—the boys were not going to get a chance to put me under house arrest.

"Well, you seem to be able to handle the crutches," said Sam. "Just don't overdo it."

Stire let me hobble out of the clinic and down its stairs. At the bottom, he picked me up and started carrying me over to the creek.

"Put me down; I can walk." I struggled in his arms.

"No. You're weak from your ordeal; in fact, you look quite pale. You can walk back after you soak your foot." I gave in. Truth be told, I didn't feel all that well.

An Alien Collective — Roxanne Barbour

At least the creek was close by, so Stire didn't have to carry me very far.

"Stire, I want to thank you for carrying me back from the ruins. I don't remember anything about our return trip."

Temmans had a strange, but obvious, smile. "No, you wouldn't. You became unconscious after about two minutes of walking. I decided you were asleep, rather than in a coma."

"You're probably right. I didn't sleep very well last night."

Thankfully, we just then arrived at the creek. I didn't want to discuss the reason I had a restless night.

* * * *

My next conscious thought was waking up covered in a blanket with my foot still in the water.

"Time for dinner," said Stire. "You need some food. It's been quite a stressful day."

With the help of my crutches, I slowly stood up. "Did you bring me a blanket?"

"Yes, you were looking a little chilled. It was probably just exhaustion. So, I left you alone for a moment and ran back for a cover. You seemed to appreciate the blanket when I put it on you."

"You're a sweetheart, Stire. I owe you big time. Now, let's get this show on the road." I started to hobble along, then stopped and looked back at Stire. "One last time?" I asked.

He just laughed, picked me up, and carried me directly to the cookhouse.

An Alien Collective – Roxanne Barbour

We made quite an impression when we entered the cookhouse. Everyone stood up and cheered and whistled, or made some sort of alien sound.
I'm so embarrassed!
"Stire, you can put me down now," I said frantically.
Stire slowly deposited me on the floor. Frakis pulled out a chair for me. "I'll get you some dinner. Any special requests?"
"Some of that grak would be nice, if it's on the menu, and a large glass of water. I am super thirsty." The pain killers must have been drying out my mouth. My crutches landed on the floor beside me.
Frakis brought me a huge plate of food, settled into her own chair, and asked, "How are you feeling?"
"Not too bad, just tired. I need a good long rest tonight, and then I'll hobble about like a maniac tomorrow."
"Only for short distances," said Stire. "You're not going back to the ruins. They're too far."
"Stire, before we start eating, perhaps you could let everyone know what you two discovered today," suggested Frakis. "And remind them that Jana's funeral is tomorrow, just before breakfast."
And that's what he did. Everyone quietly feasted on his remarks.
During our munching, I heard a lot of discussion about the ruins.
"You know, now that we've found these ruins, I can foresee a lot of requests for exploring teams." I was sure I wasn't the only one that loved to explore.
"Yes, I believe you're…"

An Alien Collective – Roxanne Barbour

Raised voices interrupted Frakis. We looked up to see an unknown Irandi standing in the cookhouse doorway.

Stire jumped up and got there at the same time as a couple of Irandi who had been eating their dinner at the closest table to the doorway. Stire spoke to the two Irandi, and then he brought the new one over to our table. He sat him down in Jana's spot.

Frakis started the questioning after the introductions were made. "Bmit, I see you have a backpack. Where have you been living?"

"I just woke up in an open area near here. There was a big box in the middle of a field, and this backpack was lying beside me." Bmit's head frantically swiveled around as he took quick looks everywhere.

Ah, Awakening Square!

"Are you hungry?" asked Frakis. At Bmit's nod, she took him up to the buffet.

After they were out of earshot, I said, "Stire, this is very strange. Why would we suddenly acquire another inhabitant for our village? What are our abductors up to?"

"I don't know, but we should be very cautious. He may be a trap of some sort; a double-crosser; who knows? Maybe he's just a replacement for Jana. Let's find out everything we can about him." We ate in silence for a moment.

We allowed Bmit a little time to eat before the bombardment started.

"Bmit, what's the last thing you remember before you woke up here?" Stire asked.

An Alien Collective – Roxanne Barbour

"I don't remember anything."

"What can you tell us about your family and your life on Irandis?" asked Frakis.

"I told you, I don't remember anything." Bmit sounded disgruntled.

The managing committee exchanged some meaningful looks. A change of subject was required.

"You have an interesting selection of food on your plate," I said.

"I found an unusual number of items I've never seen before, so I wanted to try some of them."

"I'm not sure that's such a great idea. We've already had one case of food poisoning," I commented.

"No problem. None of this food will bother me."

The food might not bother him, but his statements bothered me. I filed them away for study at another time. "Bmit, Stire, Frakis and I are the managing committee for this village. We're the ones that arrange the work duties and try to keep everything, and everyone, organized. For some unknown reason, we have all been brought here and expected to make a working society. So that's what we're trying to do. Any questions?"

"Why are we here?"

I just said it was unexplained! But I didn't say that out loud; I took a deep breath before answering. "We have no idea; our abductors don't answer any of our questions. Hopefully, we'll find out something soon. In the meantime, when you have finished eating, we'll get someone to give you an orientation tour so you know what we've accomplished so far." Bmit didn't say anything; he appeared to be in shock.

I waved Cho over. He would be excellent at showing Bmit the ropes.

After Cho took Bmit away, Jack came up to our table and asked quite a few questions about what Stire and I had found today; he wanted to update his chronicle.

"Do you guys think we should have someone from each race making a chronicle, not just Jack?" I asked.

"I don't think that's necessary," replied Frakis. "We can always translate it before we go home."

"Such an optimist," I said. Frakis's conviction hadn't transferred to me. "My main concern is that the other races could have a different perspective, an alien perspective, as it were, on everything that happens."

"Perhaps you're right, but for now I think we just need a straightforward description of the events. We'll worry about that later," Frakis continued. Stire seemed thoughtful, but he didn't speak.

"Well, I need to get back to my own journal; I'm a little behind," I said.

Gola Cho came up to our table. "Where's Bmit?"

"Don't worry, I didn't abandon him. He's outside learning the games."

"Cyn, the Irandi were wondering if you would say a few words at Jana's service tomorrow. Jana told me she considered you a friend, and you did spend a lot of time with her." Cho's green eyes were gleaming.

"Of course I will. I'm going to visit her shortly. I want to have a chat with her, one last time." Now my eyes were starting to blur; it had been a very exhausting day for me. The food had helped restore my energy a little, though.

I maneuvered myself to a standing position, and Frakis said, "Don't forget the Ballz tournament. The managing committee needs to win. Let's do it for Jana." We all smiled.

Stire and I walked over to the building where Jana was lying. She was displayed on a table and was wearing her original clothes. They looked good on her. Surrounding her were some empty food containers filled with wild flowers; the room smelled lovely.

"Do you want to be alone?" Stire asked.

"No, not really. Let's just sit down in these chairs for a while. I'm going to think about Jana, and have a little conversation with her in my head."

I thought about Jana's culture or, at least, what little I knew of it. I thought about how her life had been unexpectedly cut short. In my mind, I spoke to her and told her how I would miss her, and how I was glad to have been her friend. After about fifteen minutes, I looked up at Stire and he helped me walk back to the gaming area.

The Ballz tournament was in full swing. Much laughter and scheming was going on. The format for this tournament involved each team playing four games, and the team totals after four games would determine the winner.

There was much amusement at my hobbling up to the throw line. The managing committee, with the addition of Bmit, had a terrible first game. Then we managed to get our aim and strategy under control, and eventually won the tournament—but just barely. The tournament manager, Strik, amused us all by presenting badges. He had painted some little triangles of metal with blue paint, and had put a number 'one' on them—actually each badge had the appropriate version of 'one' on it.

"The start of my collection," announced Frakis, as she held her badge high. Everyone cheered, and the evening ended on a high note.

I gathered up some paper and a writing utensil, and then I stumbled back to our housing unit with Stire, Frakis, and Bmit. I wanted to write down my speech so I could read from it tomorrow.

"Ok, I need to get some laundry done. And then my next step will be to compose something for tomorrow's service. Hopefully, inspiration will strike."

"Cyn, I think you should focus on your speech and then get a good sleep. So, I'm going to do your laundry for you."

As I opened my mouth to protest, Frakis said, "Don't worry. You will forever be in my debt."

Reannone humor? I gave her a hug. I had never done that before.

My speech gave me a few moments of terror, but I did finish it.

I thought of how my parents would have fussed over my sprained angle; I so missed them.

Then I cried myself to sleep.

Chapter 9

In the morning, Stire, Frakis, Bmit, and I joined the stream progressing to Jana's lying-in room. I hadn't noticed last evening how large and well-lit the room was. We didn't know what it was actually meant for, but it suited today's purpose and held all of us comfortably.

The ceremony began with Irandi songs. The universal translator attempted to translate the songs, but it struggled. Since the rest of us didn't know the words, we just sat back, listened, and appreciated the singing.

I noticed Bmit standing at the back of the room. He wasn't joining the singing. Perhaps his memory loss was more complete than ours had been.

The songs were followed by some readings from their scriptures. The readings must have been a little ad hoc, as none of us had brought anything with us when we were abducted except for the clothes on our backs.

After a couple of speeches, I was motioned up to stand beside Jana's prone figure.

I took a moment to compose myself. I was a little

An Alien Collective – Roxanne Barbour

out of my element; speech-making was not a skill I had yet developed.

"Let me tell you a little about myself. My name is Cyn-Tia Silverthorne, and I'm a seventeen year-old human. Seventeen is equivalent to a young adult; an almost adult; an adult physically, but not quite an adult in terms of responsibilities. Only young adults from each race were chosen for our village. The reason I'm talking about this is because we are all in the same situation—a situation not of our making. Jana and I, and the rest of the managing committee, had some long discussions about this very topic. Why were we young adults made to participate in this experiment? I know I have no answers, but Jana kept questioning. Jana was an explorer, and would dig into everything. I think she was secretly quite excited to be part of our experience. From what I've learned so far about Irandi culture, the people of the Tine clan were known as explorers, and Jana was no exception."

I paused for a moment to catch my breath, adjust my crutches, and glance at my notes. "Jana was inquisitive by nature. Of course, she was currently studying astronomy at home, so our situation fit right into her studies. We had many discussions about numerous topics; a few of them were even a little taboo for some of us. Jana was always respectful of other opinions, and she listened very carefully to what anyone had to say. However, I'm not saying she didn't have strong opinions about a few topics." That statement created a roomful of laughter.

An Alien Collective – Roxanne Barbour

"There is an Eskimo proverb I would like to share with you. For those who do not know, the Eskimo are one of our clans."

My eyes surveyed the room; then I read from my notes. *"Perhaps they are not stars in the sky, but rather openings in heaven where the love of our lost ones pour through and shine down upon us to let us know they are happy."*

A few tears escaped down my face. "I had only known Jana for a few days, but I considered her my friend. We had a lot of laughs, and a lot of solemn moments together. She would have loved the games we have started to play; Jana did have a competitive spirit. And she would have eagerly gone to visit the new ruins we found yesterday." My crutches tapped the floor, and everyone laughed. "Jana was an exceptional person."

The room was silent. "In your memory, Jana, I wish for us all to work together to get through these trying times." I sighed, and took off my necklace; I placed it on Jana's body.

"Jana,
"Our joys will be greater
Our love will be deeper
Our lives will be fuller
Because we shared your moment."

My voice was a little husky. "Jana, I love you, and I will miss you. Please wear my necklace on your long journey." I stumbled back to Stire and Frakis.

To finish the services, the Irandi said another prayer, and then we all went for breakfast. The cooks had outdone themselves and, for the Irandi, they had some special delicacies.

After I got settled at our table—no mean task these days—I saw Cho wandering our way. Before I had a chance to speak, Cho said, "That was a wonderful speech, Cyn. It was the nicest way to send Jana off." He patted my head; that gesture surprised me.

I just smiled at him and asked, "What happens next with Jana? Do you bury her body?"

"The Irandi 'service for the dead' finishes with a cremation after a delay of one more day. So, tomorrow morning, after breakfast, we'll cremate Jana. The Irandi will build the ceremonial pyre today, if that's ok with everyone."

"Of course," Stire responded. Frakis and I just smiled and nodded. Cho sketched a salute and went back to his breakfast.

"Cho was right," said Stire. "That was a most moving speech that you gave." He touched my head.

I must have an awfully attractive head. Everyone wants to touch it.

I decided to think about that later.

"I think your gesture with the necklace was quite sweet," added Frakis. "We each have so little from our past that giving up your necklace was very special. Jana would have appreciated your gesture. Everyone else certainly did."

"It worked for me, and I really do miss her. Jana was quite a unique individual—regardless of her being alien."

Frakis commented, "Being alien doesn't really seem to be the first thing on your mind. You appear to be one of those unusual people that see personalities first—not appearances."

I didn't quite know how to respond; I hadn't thought of myself that way. My feelings and impressions had overwhelmed my consciousness. After all, I was still a teenager.

After breakfast, the troop wandered over to Awakening Square. We had been hoping for a lot, but we were disappointed again. Only food items filled the supply box.

"In my opinion, we need to send another list. We need to top up our supply of paper, at least. A couple of people have said they wanted to start a journal, and they didn't want to do it on their universal translators for fear our abductors would read it."

"I think that's a great idea. Diaries can be so therapeutic. I'm working on a journal myself, but I'm doing it on my universal translator. I have nothing to hide," I said, as I rubbed my ankle. My emotions had been all over the map recently. Writing some of my thoughts down had been therapeutic. I was starting to understand what I was feeling.

After the supplies had been stored, we assigned duties. We needed to take into account the building of the pyre for Jana, and there had been a request.

Schime and Simner, a couple of Temman females, wanted to take a long trek. They felt that we would have a better understanding of our predicament if we could map more of our surroundings.

The managing committee decided that their idea was excellent. Schime and Simner packed up two days' worth of food in their new backpacks, and we saw them off.

"You people really are nomads," I commented to Stire, when they were out of view.

"Yes, we are. It's a hard habit to break."

"Are you feeling restless yourself?" asked Frakis.

"A little bit, but since we all need to be here to open the supply box each day, none of us are going anywhere for very long," responded Stire. "And Cyn is not going to the ruins today. It really is too far to hobble." With that last comment, he really brought out my sulkiness.

"Well, how about a short walk to that hill just north of here? Am I allowed to go that far?" I pointed out the hill I was referring to.

"Yes, but not alone. No one goes anywhere alone, remember?"

Frakis looked at us and said, "I think I'll do some gardening today. Our plot is developing nicely, and some of the seeds are starting to sprout. The gardening crew wants to get more planted." With a little wave, she picked up her pack and started walking towards the gardens. "I'll see you guys later."

"And what is the nature of our expedition?" asked Stire, as he proceeded to fill one pack with enough supplies for both of us.

"We're looking for more ruins. I love ruins—my

An Alien Collective – Roxanne Barbour

ankle doesn't, but I do—and I'm hoping there'll be a nice surprise around that small hill. It seems to beckon."

I was already feeling more cheerful.

In the distance, the hill glistened in the sunlight. It appeared to be covered with low vegetation that was approaching a dark green color. Calling it a hill was an overstatement. The mound of dirt was maybe only two stories high and surrounded by brush.

Again, the sun was brilliant. A few drops of rain would have been welcome, though; they would have freshened the air. We were going to have to cross the stream to reach the hill, so I seized the chance to chill my ankle for a bit. The cooling was quickening my healing process.

"So what should we name this hill we're going to search?" asked Stire while we sat by the creek.

"Let's come up with something positive-sounding; maybe *Mount Everest* or *Mountain of the Gods*, or *The Hill of Discovery*."

"I like *The Hill of Discovery*," responded Stire. "We may get other ideas when we actually do our search."

"You're right. I like *The Hill of Discovery* too." Even though it was shortly after breakfast, I had a bite to eat while my ankle rested.

"And, don't forget, we also need a name for our village, although it's going to be tricky to find a name that means something to everyone." Stire had a depth of understanding about our situation that amazed me.

"Let's move along while my ankle is feeling good. I don't want it to stiffen up."

An Alien Collective – Roxanne Barbour

The way towards the Hill of Discovery was easy walking. There wasn't a distinct path like there had been to yesterday's ruins; nevertheless, the slope was gentle and easy to traverse. We walked through meadows covered in flowers. The majority of the foliage had a light purple hue. There were no birds or butterflies; the strangeness of no winged animals of any sort continued.

The slope steepened slightly to the top of the hill. It was easy enough for me to manage with my crutches. The view from the top of the hill was amazing. The village and the lake were obvious, and I also thought I saw the ruins from yesterday.

With no discoveries on the hill top, we continued our search around the base. My enthusiasm hadn't diminished.

An unusual amount of brush hugged the hill around its perimeter, but that didn't deter me. I looked behind each piece of brush. To my annoyance, the brush was very prickly.

"Stire, I think I see a little hole behind this brush. Can you help me get it out of the way, please?" I called out to him. He was about thirty feet ahead of me. Holding on to crutches made it hard for me to actually pull out any foliage.

Stire pulled some of the brush out of the way, the opening was larger than I had realized.

In fact, when Stire threw the last bit of brush aside, we found the opening tall enough for us to get through.

"I wish I had a flashlight," I said. I desperately wanted to see inside.

An Alien Collective – Roxanne Barbour

"I'm going to take a couple steps forward. You stay behind me," suggested Stire. As he hesitantly entered the cave, there was a burst of light.

"Let me see, let me see!"

Stire moved forward and to the right so I could stand beside him.

I was amazed! The cave was full of electronic equipment; racks and racks of it. All of it appeared to be in working order, as there were lights flashing throughout the room. The cave was about twenty feet square, and it was crammed full.

Chapter 10

"Stire, what is this?" I was anxious; something about this situation was strange. A room full of modern technology was not what I had expected to find during our exploring.

"I think we've found our abductors' control room. This must be where they keep an eye on us, and where they make sure our village is running smoothly." Stire sounded a little apprehensive.

"Why are you worried?"

"Because I don't think we were meant to find this cave. Let's get out of here, and then we can figure out what to do. We need to leave before someone shows up and discovers us." Stire helped me out of the cave, and we walked a little ways away.

"Do you think we should continue exploring around the perimeter?" I asked.

"Not today. We need to get back to the village and discuss this situation with Frakis, and perhaps a few others. My mind is churning with options. I don't know how upset our abductors would be if they found out we had been in the cave."

"I guess you're right. But, on the other hand, I would like to confront them."

It's time they stopped hiding!

As best we could, Stire and I covered the entrance with the brush he had pulled away. Our walk back to the village was mostly silent. We had a lot to think about.

Upon our arrival, we found Frakis in the cookhouse helping with the preparation of our next meal. My suggestion to sit down and have a snack with us was readily accepted.

"What's up? You both look so serious. You didn't hurt yourself again, did you Cyn?" For some reason, Frakis found that amusing.

"Actually, my foot is much better; I haven't taken a pain killer all day. No, we need to tell you about what we found today."

Discussing the cave and the massive amount of instrumentation we had found didn't take long. We didn't have a huge amount of detail, since we had bolted from the cave almost immediately. Frakis got a thoughtful look on her face.

"I think you were right to be worried about what our abductors would do if they found out that someone had trespassed. Our situation seems more long term as each day passes." She paused for a moment. "Today, I've been thinking about Cyn's comment about cameras being everywhere. I bet they added cameras and microphones to our new backpacks, since they must have been horrified to learn they didn't prevent Jana's death. Our village is most likely saturated with cameras."

"And, if there are microphones, we are truly guinea pigs," I added.

Stire and Frakis looked at me strangely. I had to laugh—new words challenged the universal translator.

"Oh, I guess you don't know what a guinea pig is. A guinea pig is a small animal that is sometimes used in scientific experiments. And the analogy is that we are guinea pigs in our abductors' experiments."

"So what should we do? Should we try and find all of the cameras and destroy them?" Frakis asked.

"That's certainly one possibility. But how much do you want to bet they would just replace them if we did that?" asked Stire.

"No bet, but I do have a thought. Why don't we destroy every one of them we can find here in the cookhouse? That way, at least, we would have a private meeting room large enough for everyone. A couple of us could stay here all night to watch out for retaliatory activity from our abductors," I suggested.

"Good plan," commented Frakis.

It only took a short time to search through the dining area, and half a dozen cameras were discovered. Although I thought the dining room would have been an obvious place for microphones, we didn't find any. We were alone in the room, so our actions remained a secret.

"How soon do you think our abductors will notice that they can't monitor the dining area?" I asked.

An Alien Collective – Roxanne Barbour

"Hopefully sometime today," replied Frakis. "I want to confront them. By the way, I'm staying here tonight. Who's with me?"

After a short discussion, all three of us decided to spend the night in the dining area. I hadn't paid much attention to the benches attached to the inside walls, but Frakis pointed out they would make adequate beds. We just needed our own linens.

"You know, this is just strange. On one hand, they seem to want us to become self-sufficient, like growing vegetables and butchering meat. But, on the other hand, they have control rooms, listening and watching devices, and who knows what else. I don't understand the purpose of our situation." I knew I sounded frustrated.

Before Stire or Frakis had a chance to respond, people started to arrive for dinner, so we curtailed our conversation.

Dinner began as a lively affair; the atmosphere was quite positive. The day appeared to have been productive for all, and when Stire announced that we would have a contest to name our village, the conversations exploded.

"And don't forget to give an explanation on why your entry would be appropriate for the village name. Have your proposals in by lunch time tomorrow, and we'll vote at dinner."

A few came up to our table to grab some paper that Frakis had conveniently thought to provide. When we were alone again, Gola Cho got our attention.

"I wanted to let you know I found something a little

strange this afternoon. After I had finished my kitchen duties, I felt the need for some exercise. In my previous wanderings, I had noticed that one of the empty lots in our unnamed village looked a little peculiar. I thought I found a pattern in the ground cover. So I got a shovel and started digging." Cho grinned. "If you would follow me, I'll show you what I've discovered."

Cho had certainly piqued my interest. We put our dishes away and followed Cho to his empty lot. In just a few moments, we arrived at the open area. The pattern in the vegetation was obvious; there was something just below the surface. Where he had been digging, there appeared to be slightly curving metal lines in the dirt.

"I bet this pattern continues and we get concentric circles," I said. "Let's clean out the remaining cover and see what we find."

Stire and Cho went to gather up some shovels, while Frakis ran back to the gaming area to get additional helpers.

The digging went quickly. However, I had to watch from the sidelines. Trying to shovel with crutches and a sprained ankle was out of the question. After about an hour, a series of concentric circles were uncovered. The diameter of the largest circle was around twenty feet.

"This looks strikingly like the bottom of the supply box," commented Stire. "I wonder if it does the same thing, but on a larger scale."

"What do you mean?" asked Frakis.

I didn't know what Stire was getting at, either.

"The coil in the supply box brings us items. We also know it sends them some other place because our notes disappeared. Perhaps this coil does the same thing, but with large objects, or more objects at the same time."

"But how is it operated? For that matter, how is the supply box operated?" I asked.

"The supply box is most likely operated from our end when we close it. There is probably a switch in the lid. At the other end, our abductors will have some sort of switch too. Maybe even a control panel."

I wasn't convinced by Stire's statements. "Perhaps; but what was this coil used for?"

"Since it is much larger than the supply box, it was probably used in the construction of the village. Quite a number of supplies would have been needed for a project of this size," said Stire.

"Maybe this is a one-way coil," Frakis said.

"Unlikely. The workers would have to go back and forth; I couldn't see them living here while they built the village."

"True. So what are we going to do? Just throw things on the rings?" *I need some action, here!*

Talking ceased while we considered our options.

The first thing we tried was a shovel; it went nowhere. Then, a Reannone volunteered to stand on the rings. He stood there patiently, but nothing happened.

"Stire, you must be right about a control panel. Now, where would we find one?" I asked. I looked around the empty plot. The only things visible were some small bushes in one corner.

An Alien Collective – Roxanne Barbour

Frakis and Stire saw me gazing at the bushes, so they walked over there to poke about. Shortly, Stire began pulling out some of the greenery. Even from my distance, it was obvious that daylight was bouncing off a metal panel. The rest of the crowd ran to Stire and Frakis while I hobbled my way over.

"Cyn, you were right about where the controls would be," Stire said. Even though I had only looked in the direction of the brush, my thoughts had apparently been quite obvious.

"So what are we going to do? Is the control panel self-explanatory?" Even though I liked math and computers, I really wasn't an engineering type.

"The control panel looks fairly simple, and it seems to have power—although I don't know where it comes from. We're going to have to do some experiments to understand how it works."

"Ok, so I'm just going to sit here on the ground and watch you guys sweat." My ankle was killing me; it was a relief to sit down. Perhaps I had overdone the exercise today.

Stire first experimented with one of the bushes he had ripped out of the ground. The bush disappeared. When he tried to bring it back, it appeared after a minute. Stire then successfully tried the same sequence on a shovel.

So far, so good!

"So what's the next item you're going to try with the coil?" I asked.

"I don't know. I think perhaps..."

A Reannone, Jeena a Simo, interrupted Stire. "I would like to volunteer. I want to see what our abductors look like, and I want to enlighten them with my opinion about this experiment of theirs." Jeena fiddled with her yellow scarf.

"I'm sure we would all like to give them a piece of our minds," I said.

Frakis hesitantly said, "Why would you want to cut out some of your brains?"

"Oh, it's just an expression. It means that we very strongly want to tell them what's going through our minds."

Frakis laughed. "You have no idea the images I was seeing!"

I continued, "Anyway, I don't think we should experiment with a person just yet. Why don't we try again with more questions? That would be a better next step, and we just might irritate them into answering."

Chapter 11

On a high note, our questions were not returned immediately. We would be impatiently waiting for a response.

The evening wound down quickly. The managing committee hung around until we were the last ones in the cookhouse. We didn't want anyone to know we were going to be camping out.

We hustled back to our housing unit and picked up our supplies for the night. Bmit was nowhere to be found, so we were successful in hiding our actions.

After settling down in the cookhouse, we chatted for a little while; it wasn't long before we fell asleep.

I didn't feel like I dreamt much. Some nights, my dreaming, since we had arrived, had been very weird—even stranger than the situation we were in.

I awoke fairly early in the morning. The cooks were just beginning to arrive. They needed a couple of hours before breakfast time to start their daily tasks. Our presence was quite a surprise to them.

Stire and Frakis woke up about the same time I did. Perhaps the noise from the kitchen staff was a factor. We looked at each other, and then wandered surreptitiously around the dining room. All cameras had reappeared.

"Did anyone see or hear anything last night?" I asked.

They both indicated they had not.

"They must have knocked us out with some gas or something," I said.

"Well, they did something. I never sleep that soundly, and there should have been some noise when they replaced the cameras," added Frakis.

"Yes, our abductors definitely put us out of commission for the night." Stire sounded annoyed.

"Let's go get cleaned up and return our linens. I think breakfast will have some very lively discussions," replied Frakis.

Bmit wasn't in our housing unit; perhaps he was at the cookhouse.

At the cookhouse, Frakis was immediately approached by a Reannone and an Irandi. The three of them had a long and animated discussion. Then Frakis slowly walked over to our table. To me, it was apparent that she was worried about something.

"Frakis, what's the matter?"

"A very delicate situation has occurred—a Reannone and an Irandi wish to mate. And they have asked that we make a ruling on the situation."

A Reannone and an Irandi? Is mating even possible

for mixed species? Could they conceive? My mind was flooded with questions.

"Why do we have to make a ruling?" I said carefully.

"Well, for one thing, mating between different alien species has never happened before. We've never even met any aliens."

You're not the only one!

"And people on Reannone who wish to mate must get the permission of their families. To top this situation, there is a slight taboo about mating between the different clans, although this has happened occasionally in the past. Can you imagine how taboo different species would be? All in all, this is a unique situation."

"And I expect we're the closest thing to family," I commented. "So it's up to us to make a decision?"

"Yes, that seems to be the reasoning. I never expected to be giving permission at my age."

Frakis rubbed her forehead. If she were human, I would have decided she had a massive headache.

"Could we ask them to chill out for a bit?" I asked.

"What do you mean 'chill out'?" asked Frakis.

"To back away from the relationship. We've only been together about seven days. Isn't that too soon for a serious relationship to develop? Their emotions are probably suspect. They need to stand back and reassess their feelings."

"I think seven days is a reasonable length of time for a relationship to develop," commented Stire. "However, I do agree that we don't know our future. Perhaps we'll all be sent home in a couple of days. What then?

How would the two of them handle a complete separation after a short time together?"

"I think Stire's right, Frakis. After breakfast, perhaps you could have a chat with them and point out the instability of our situation. At least suggest that they give us a few days before moving their relationship ahead. Do you think they'd go along with that?"

"I don't know; they seemed pretty serious. I do agree with both of your assessments, so I will try and be very persuasive." Frakis sighed. "It's not going to be easy. Young adult emotions are volatile; for all races, I'm sure."

I didn't know what to think. Did their pairing occur because of our situation? Obviously, to some degree, but were they really meant for each other?

Frakis continued, "I think it's time to summarize to everyone what happened at the coil yesterday, and what we had hoped to accomplish staying in the cookhouse last night. But let's not mention the cave you guys found. I want to take a look at it first."

After Stire wound up his speech, he came back to our table. Then Bmit appeared.

"You almost missed breakfast," Frakis said.

"There was no activity in our housing unit, so I just kept sleeping. You guys are really quiet. Perhaps you could wake me up next time, if I'm not up and about?"

"Certainly. You'll probably get used to our routine, though," said Frakis.

Just as we were getting up to go to the supply box,

An Alien Collective – Roxanne Barbour

a couple of Irandi burst into the cookhouse. "Jana is missing!"

I couldn't believe what I had just heard. "What do you mean *missing*?"

"She's disappeared from her resting place. We went there to carry her to her funeral pyre, and she's just gone. What are we supposed to do?"

The managing committee rushed over to the building where Jana had been lying—most of us rushed, that is. Everything was intact. There were no obvious clues to what had taken place. Jana was just missing.

"I don't see how any animal could have gotten in and carried her off," said Frakis. "And no one here would have played any trick like that."

"No, I think it's our captors," I answered. "I don't know what they're up to, but I don't like it. They shouldn't interfere with the Irandi customs. Now what are we going to do?"

"An inspection of the entire village would probably be in order. Perhaps they stored Jana some other place, although I doubt it. Right now, though, we need to get to the supply box. Everyone will be waiting for us, and we need to see if there's any response to our questions."

We were, indeed, the last ones to arrive at the supply box. Upon opening the box, no papers were visible. We did get a lot of supplies, though.

"Oh, well, maybe there are some answers at the coil," said Stire. "But, before we go there, let's get everyone organized for the day."

Since we were settling into a routine, it was relatively easy to arrange the duties; people were discovering which activities suited them best. We arranged for a group to do a thorough search of our village for Jana.

Jeena followed us to the coil. It was difficult to stop her; we knew what she wanted.

"I'm going to try another item through the portal," said Stire. "Additional testing is required." Stire sent his backpack through the coil, and successfully brought it back. The big decision was upon us.

"I really want to try this," said the tall, black-eyed Jeena.

"Anything could go wrong," replied Frakis, "seriously wrong."

"I know. Your experiments have been successful so far, though."

"All except the questions we sent." Apparently, that was a pet peeve of mine.

"I'm sure our abductors kept those papers deliberately. They're probably making some grand scrapbook out of everything we do. I do think your next step is to send a person," Jeena responded.

"We're reluctant to put anyone into a possibly dangerous situation," Stire said.

"And I think we need to see what's on the other side," replied Jeena.

So we let her go.

Stire couldn't bring her back. He tried and tried.

"Stire, you have to stop. We'll try again later in the day. You did your best, but our captors are playing with us," said Frakis.

An Alien Collective – Roxanne Barbour

Stire looked so crestfallen.

To take our minds off Jeena for a little while, we decided it was time to explore the cave. We packed up some supplies for the day, but just announced we were off to do some exploring. The knowledge of the cave would continue to be confined to the managing committee.

Our walk to the cave was not relaxed; we were very concerned about Jeena. A rest at the creek was in order, so I could soak my ankle. It was much better today, and I was actually walking on it unassisted for short periods. The crutches had sped up my recovery. We decided to rest in our favorite spot by the creek.

Frakis asked, "What are we going to do? We need to get the attention of our captors. We need to go home."

"I agree that our first step is to get their attention," said Stire. "However, we don't want to annoy them so much they decide to terminate all of us."

"That's awfully negative," I said. I couldn't believe Stire had uttered those words; he must be under a lot of pressure. I continued, "What we need to do is go against some of their wishes. For example, we were told each housing unit had to have a person from each race. What if we mix that up?"

"Or maybe we should take down all the surveillance equipment we can find? There are probably a lot of them throughout the village. Actually, there's probably one in each of our own rooms. Having some privacy might be nice," suggested Frakis, looking at both of us.

Stire looked at me and said, "Actually, that suggestion is quite appropriate. We could look in the camera and say something about privacy as we take each one down. We could leave the ones in our village for now, until we see what our captors do."

We tabled our discussion and started walking towards the cave.

"You know what we forgot to do today," I said. "We forgot to send anyone over to those ruins we found for further exploration. I'm really curious about the previous inhabitants. Were they our abductors?"

"Actually, we decided to leave the ruins alone until you were up to walking there. I know you're an explorer type, as are Stire and I, but most of the others are still frightened about our situation and don't want too many unanswered questions. So, we're leaving the exploring until you're ready," replied Frakis.

"As for who they were, those ruins were pretty old," said Stire. "I think it's another race entirely. However, since we haven't seen our abductors, I could be completely wrong. But I do think it's important to go back and do a thorough search. The city isn't that big—it's only the size our village. A thorough exploration wouldn't take very long."

"Well, I'm game, and here's our cave coming up," I said.

After the brush was pulled away, we were surprised and disappointed to find that the entrance had been sealed. There was absolutely no way we could access the cave.

An Alien Collective – Roxanne Barbour

"Apparently we triggered some alarm when we were here," said Stire. "So our abductors closed it up."

"That's quite disappointing," said Frakis. "I'd been looking forward to poking about their equipment. We might have been able to figure something out. You know, the machinery is still in there. With my antennae, I can hear some of the higher frequencies the equipment is emitting."

That surprised me.

"I do have a question; did you search the entire base of this hill for other caves?"

"No, we didn't. When we discovered this cave, we quickly removed ourselves and went back to the village. We were hoping we hadn't been noticed," I replied.

But apparently we had been.

"If you're up to it, I think we should explore the rest. They may have been sloppy and left something else for us to find, and I may be able to hear if there is another entrance to this cave," Frakis said.

"Ever the optimist," I commented.

"Did you name this place?" Frakis asked. She interrupted herself, "Of course you did, Cyn; you name everything."

I was slightly embarrassed. "Ok, I did. Unless you have any objections, this is officially *The Hill of Discovery*." Frakis was starting to understand me quite well.

Frakis just laughed.

We explored the rest of the base of the hill. It took quite a while because there was a lot of brush to look behind. Much to our surprise, we found another cave.

An Alien Collective – Roxanne Barbour

This cave, however, did not have any motion detecting lights. Visibility was at a minimum.

"I can't see anything," said Frakis. "And I don't think it's wise to proceed in the dark. We need some kind of illumination." She clearly wanted to explore a cave; any cave.

"The only thing that comes to mind is some kind of torch. I know the cooks have some gadgets that produce a spark for lighting the fires, so we could borrow one of those. Now we just need to create a torch that will last for some time when lit." Stire was clearly hard at work trying to find a solution.

"We can think about that on the way back. We still have a little bit of unexplored hillside, so let's finish that up before we head back." Frakis was clearly eager to explore.

However, the rest of our exploration turned out to be uneventful; we found nothing of significance. The countryside continued to amaze me, though. The meadows contained gorgeous little flowers in varying colors. My urge to garden kept reappearing.

Our walk back to the village was a quiet affair. Stire and Frakis were as lost in thought, as was I.

I needed to figure out what we could do to get the attention of our captors. Why did our abductors feel they had the right to uproot all of us; to remove us from our families and friends; to transport us to another planet? If nothing else, we needed some explanations. I didn't cope well with being in the dark. I wanted logical explanations, and I wanted them now. However, I had to laugh at myself; I had discovered I wasn't as patient as I thought I was. At least one good thing had developed as a result of our situation: I was learning about alien civilizations, and I was making new friends. This was not something I had ever envisioned.

And I need to examine my relationship with Stire; I am so confused.

Approaching our village, Frakis said, "I'm going to have a rest. I'm feeling quite tired; I don't think I slept very well last night."

"That's a good idea. My ankle's killing me," I added.

"You should have said something," Stire said. "I could have carried you."

Frakis appeared to stifle a laugh; I didn't know what her problem was.

"Thanks, but I decided I needed the exercise. My ankle will never get better if I don't keep working on it. However, a rest right now will be most delightful."

It took me about three seconds to fall asleep. I don't think I even dreamt, because the next thing I knew, Frakis was shaking me awake.

"Such a sleepy head! We've been trying to wake you for a couple of minutes."

Stire and Frakis were standing over me.

"If we don't get going, we're going to be late for dinner. And tonight's a big night; we're going to name our village."

I quickly washed up and we went to dinner. My ankle was doing a little protest dance, though; perhaps I had *overdone* it today.

An Alien Collective – Roxanne Barbour

The proposed names for our village were sitting on our table. We put each name on a separate sheet of paper and passed the stack around. During dinner, each person wrote their name on one of the sheets of paper.

"It's interesting to see," I said as we watched, "that no name seems to be favored by a particular race; although some of the names aren't getting many votes."

"You're right. And your idea of writing each name in the four languages made things a lot easier for everyone," replied Frakis. "And Stire's notion of having a second vote on the top three is going to help narrow down the choices. This is going well."

We ate for a while in silence and then tallied the votes.

"The top three are obvious," Frakis commented, "although I don't understand the significance of the names that were chosen, but I guess that doesn't matter. Ok, let's have a second secret ballot on the three finalists—Reit, Keene, and Spider."

The amusement was obvious when everyone heard the list. Who would name a village after a game?

"You know, it's quite delightful to have such a selection of fruit for dessert," commented Frakis while we were waiting for everyone to cast their votes. "Did we find a new supply?"

"No, these were from the original grove of trees we found. To make it safer, though, the engineering crew developed some defensive weapons. We now have a collection of spears and bows and arrows," Stire answered.

An Alien Collective – Roxanne Barbour

"That's quick work; we do have some very talented people in our group. Perhaps we could use some of the fruit to ferment some beverages," suggested Frakis.

"Yes, a glass of wine would be nice occasionally." I wondered if we had any vintners in our group, or whatever the alien equivalent was. The cooks had been making various kinds of breads, so there must be some sort of yeast available.

"I was sad to hear that Jana was nowhere to be found in the village," I said.

"Yes, the Irandi would have liked some closure," Stire responded.

Momentarily, the votes came back to our table, and I announced the winner.

"The name of our village has been decided. We now reside in the village of *Reit*." There were numerous outbursts. I wondered how our universal translator translated *Reit*. I continued, "And as a consolation to our third place winner, let's go and have a game of Spider!"

We walked outside and Frakis asked, "What does *Reit* mean?"

"I can answer that," I said. "Jack, our human that is studying journalism, had the brilliant idea of taking the first letter of each race name and combining them. It took him a little while, apparently, to get the right arrangement of letters that could be spoken in all languages. So 'Reit' is sort of based on English and stands for 'Reanno, Earth, Irandis, and Temma'."

"That was quite clever of him."

"Yes, but I think he also put on his politician's hat and spent some considerable amount of time convincing others that it was the democratic choice."

Frakis just laughed and then soberly said, "Let's go check the coil and see if Jeena's returned."

We had suggested this morning that everyone check the coil, when they had a moment, to see if Jeena had returned. So far, there had been no sign of her.

At the coil, Stire sent an object away and attempted to bring it back. The object came back successfully, but there was no Jeena with it.

"I'm really starting to worry about Jeena," I said. "I have a bad feeling about this."

"Don't worry. I think our abductors have her and are talking to her about our activities. We are a bit of a nuisance, and they want to know what we're going to do next."

I could tell Frakis was trying to reassure me; however, I wasn't convinced she really believed what she was saying. "Well, since we don't know what we're going to do next, Jeena certainly can't tell them anything." I scowled. "I think we should annoy our abductors again. Why don't we do what we were talking about before; let's remove the cameras from our housing units."

Stire and Frakis perked up at my suggestion.

"Oh, good suggestion," Stire said. "But let's do it a little differently. Instead of removing the cameras, let's just cover them with some of that tape we have. That will really confuse them."

We went back to the gaming area and announced

An Alien Collective – Roxanne Barbour

our decision. It was greeted with great enthusiasm.

After a long game of Spider, which involved the whole village, we headed home. Someone from each housing unit had a length of tape. Tomorrow's breakfast discussions should prove to be interesting.

"Except for Jeena, I think this has been a successful day. The village spirit is picking up," I said.

"Yes. And the little act of defiance we are going to perpetrate is helping to consolidate that spirit," added Frakis.

It took a while, but we found a camera in every room of our housing unit. Covering them up with tape was done quickly.

"Now that completes our successful day," said Frakis. What I assumed was a yawn escaped from her mouth. "I'll see you guys tomorrow."

I said goodnight and turned to Stire.

Before I had a chance to speak, Stire said, "Let's sit down on the couch for a moment; I have something I want to discuss with you." On the couch, he turned to face me. "This is awkward for me, Cyn-Tia, but I need to say it. I have discovered that I have feelings for you."

Chapter 12

I will always remember this moment.
 Stire took my hand in his. "I have so many emotions flooding my mind right now, and most of them involve you. I like to be near you, and I love how you think through our problems. Most of all, I love to touch you and hug you, and carry you around when you can't walk." We both laughed. "I hope this isn't too much for you; it's certainly overwhelming for me. I never expected to have feelings for an alien. Actually, I never expected to meet an alien, but I had to tell you how I felt." He looked at me anxiously.
 What am I supposed to say?
 "Stire, I think I have some feelings for you, too. But I am so mixed up because of our situation that I am having a hard time understanding my emotions. You're certainly special to me, but I'm not sure how far it goes. For the next little while, can we just be very good friends?" That was as far as I wanted to commit for the moment.

Stire didn't say anything, but when I put my arms out to him, he gathered me in. We sat together for a few moments, and then we went to our rooms to get some rest.

At this point, a conversation with my mother would have been wonderful.

In the end, I didn't know about Stire, but restful was not how I would have described my night.

* * * *

The next morning, I was starving. It seemed like my uncomfortable night had added to my normally robust appetite. Surveying the available breakfast items, I thought I saw something new. I reached to take a portion…and found myself on the floor.

Someone pushed me!

Stire helped me to my feet. "Are you alright, Cyn?"

"Yes, but I think I made a mess." I knew I made a mess; my tray of food littered the floor. "Someone pushed me, Stire."

"Yes, I know." I watched Stire rush after a Temman that was walking away. They both went out the cookhouse door.

Frakis touched my shoulder, and then she gave me a tray. "Get some breakfast," she suggested.

I glanced down at the floor and saw my mess being cleaned up. "Jack, let me do that. I made this mess."

"Don't worry about it. We all saw what happened."

Frakis gently turned me towards the food.

Stire soon joined us at our table. It was quite obvious he didn't want to discuss the situation.

An Alien Collective – Roxanne Barbour

To top breakfast off, I was convinced Frakis could sense our discomfort. It felt like she knew exactly what was going on. Being ever the tactful one, she ignored our obvious feelings and just chattered about the things we needed to do today.

An Irandi came up to our table while we were eating; it was Kane Kene.

"What's up, Kene?" I asked. She looked a little nervous. Maybe she was wondering if we had made a decision about her and Brik becoming a serious couple; like the managing committee could now be impartial about that situation.

"The Irandi were discussing your committee. And, ah, um, we think the committee should have an Irandi member, to represent all Irandi here in the village. We know that Irandi DNA is not needed for the supply box any more, but we think we should have a say in the decisions." Kene looked relieved when she finished her speech.

"Actually, that's a very good idea," responded Frakis. "Give us a few moments to think about it. Approach us when we have finished our breakfast."

Watching Kene walk back to her table, my thoughts turned to Jana.

"That's not such a bad idea," Stire said. "It makes perfect sense to have some Irandi representation. Any disagreement?"

I couldn't argue with them. I missed Jana, but it made complete sense to have an Irandi help us manage our village of four races. "Who should it be? Should we pick someone?" I asked.

Bmit interrupted, "Since I am living in the managing committee's housing unit, it should most likely be me."

How were we going to handle this? Bmit was even stranger than the other Irandi.

"Actually, since you have been with us only a short time, I think one of the original Irandi would have a better feel on how our village is managed." That was as tactful a response as I could manage. Our table was silent for a moment, and then Bmit stomped off. "Ok, that didn't go very well," I said.

"Perhaps not, but it was a wise comment," said Frakis. "So, who should we choose?"

"I think it should be Cho. He seems to be the most level-headed of the Irandi I have met," answered Stire.

At the end of our meal, we let Kene know that we would accept Cho as part of the managing committee. She ran off to get him. Very shortly, Cho joined us.

"Welcome to the managing committee," I said to Cho. "We're happy to have some Irandi input. How are you feeling about this?"

"I really don't think you guys need my help. You have been doing a great job making all the hard decisions, but perhaps a little input on the Irandi culture will be of benefit."

"Well spoken, Cho. Don't worry; we're going to put you to work immediately." We all laughed. There was never a shortage of things to decide or do.

"First on our agenda, after we have discussed a few things over breakfast, is to go and open the supply box.

An Alien Collective – Roxanne Barbour

I know you don't need to be there, but you should get used to our routine. Also, we need you to help us get the supplies organized and divvy up today's tasks."

I continued, "There is one tricky situation you will have to deal with. Bmit wanted to be the Irandi representative, but we told him 'no' since he has only been here a little while." I smiled. "Since the managing committee is supposed to be housed together, you're going to have to arrange trading rooms with him."

"Nothing easy to start with!" Cho said, but he did add a smile.

The supply box did not have any surprises today. We found a pile of food items and a small stack of paper. Those were certainly necessary items, but there was nothing new.

Once the supplies were back at the cookhouse, we assigned the day's tasks. Today's work included covering every camera we could find, sending a crew for lots more fruit, replenishing the herd of grak, and continuing with the gardens.

After eight days, the gardens were sprouting like crazy. We would soon have some fresh greens. It turned out that the alien 'greens' were also, generally, green. This was a similarity I had not expected. We also convinced a couple of the engineering committee to create some torches.

Our next step was to go to the coil. We needed to do some more experimenting. Much to our surprise, and excitement, Jeena was there. She was sitting on the ground and looking stunned.

An Alien Collective – *Roxanne Barbour*

"Jeena, are you all right?" I asked. Frakis and I helped her up. She shook a little, and her face was pale.

"I guess so. What happened to me?" She looked around. "Oh, now I remember; I volunteered to go through the coil. When was that?"

"Yesterday. Let's get you back to the cookhouse; I'm sure you're very hungry," said Frakis.

"Oh yes, I am. I don't remember eating since I left here. Of course, I don't remember much at all."

Since Jeena was looking quite frail and there was a wheelbarrow sitting by the coil, Stire put her in it and ran back to the cookhouse. I followed along at a slower pace.

The cooks quickly scrounged up some breakfast. It didn't take Jeena long to start eating. We were anxious to ask her some questions, but we bided our time.

While we were waiting for her to relax a little, we discussed some of the changes since she had been away. The main two topics were the covering up of the cameras in the housing units and the addition of Cho to the managing committee.

"Adding an Irandi to the managing committee was a very good idea," Jeena said. "And I do like the fact that you are expanding the camera denial—a little privacy sometimes would be nice."

I wondered what Jeena wanted privacy for. Probably nothing unusual—we all needed peace and quiet once in a while.

"So, Jeena, can you tell us anything about your absence? Even just a little thing or two," Frakis asked

An Alien Collective – Roxanne Barbour

gently. That's what I loved about Frakis: she was such a compassionate person.

"I remember the actual experience of…I don't know what you want to call it—the experience of leaving, I guess. I felt a tingle all over my body and then nothing. I could feel time passing a little, but I didn't feel much else. Sorry."

"It must have been such a traumatic experience for you," I said.

"Not really. I don't think I was conscious for most of it, honestly. I just feel really tired right now."

"Just a couple more questions," said Frakis, "and then we'll let you get some rest. Did you hear or see anything during your absence from Reit?"

"Reit? What's that?"

"Sorry, that's what we named our village last night. It stands for each of our planets—Reanno, Earth, Temma, and Irandis," said Frakis.

"That's kind of sweet. Anyway, as for anything else, I thought I heard voices once in a while, and I am pretty sure I saw some bright lights. Really, I don't remember much. I didn't see our abductors, and I didn't see any alien landscapes. I don't know what else to tell you."

"That's an excellent start," said Stire. "And I think you need some rest now. Do you want us to take you back to your housing unit? Do you want to be checked over by a medic?"

"No, that's not necessary. I feel quite a lot better with some food in me, but I'll certainly be sleeping for a few hours. I'll see you all this evening." At that, Jeena got up and walked out of the cookhouse. She was a lot steadier than when we had found her at the coil.

"Guys, let's go over to the store room and check out the progress on our torches," Frakis said.

The engineers were having a couple of problems, but we patiently waited while they sorted them out. In a little while, we had the torches we needed and a means to light them.

"It's almost lunch time. Over a meal, we can tell Cho all about our decisions and how we come to them, although he may think we're kind of spacey."

"I would never think anything like that about the managing committee. After all, I am now a part of it." I was coming to the conclusion Cho had a wicked sense of humor.

While we were bringing Cho up to date on our activities, the scouts, Simner and Schime, arrived back at the village. They were looking a little tired and a whole lot hungry. After they washed up and grabbed some food, they sat down with us. We let them eat for a few moments, and then I couldn't contain my eagerness any longer.

"What exciting things did you find?" I asked.

"We certainly saw a great deal of the countryside. We found a bigger lake and creek than what we have here. And we found a stand of trees with some fruit that is significantly different from what we have eaten so far. We did bring some samples back, but we haven't tried them yet." Simner paused for a moment.

"Were there any predators hanging around the fruit

trees?" asked Frakis. That question was on everyone's mind.

"No, and we didn't see any during the rest of our scouting expedition. But," Schime seemed particularly amused about what she was going to say next, "we did see some two-legged ones."

"What do you mean?" asked Stire. Her smile made us all curious.

"We found another village, just like ours—full of Temmans, Irandi, Reannone, and humans. In fact, the village was designed in exactly the same way as ours," added Schime.

"Really? An exact duplicate?" I was astonished.

"Yes. And there appeared to be the same number of people that our village has. But, you know, they don't seem to be as well organized. We saw a lot of people just sitting around the village doing nothing." Simner didn't seem impressed.

Perhaps the managing committee had been doing a better job than I thought at running the village.

"Did you talk to anyone?" asked Frakis.

"No. We decided to just observe for a while, and then report back. Perhaps we're supposed to be isolated from this other group. Schime and I discussed it, but we thought the managing committee would like to decide what to do. Actually, we didn't get a very comfortable feeling about the group. It was like they were just coexisting, not cooperating with each other. Mind you, that was just an impression we gathered from a distance. Perhaps it isn't true."

An Alien Collective – Roxanne Barbour

"Nice work. We'll debrief you more later on. Right now, you look like you could use some rest," commented Frakis.

"Yes, we could. We spent all last night and this morning getting back here."

After Schime and Simner left, I turned to the others, "So what are we going to do about this other village? Obviously, our abductors set up more than one. Do you think there are more than two?"

The silence around the table was profound. Cho was tapping the table while he thought, and Frakis was rubbing her antennae. All I wanted to do was lay my head on the table, but I resisted.

"This is a very surprising development," said Stire. "I hadn't even imagined that our abductors would have other villages like ours. What are they up to?"

"I don't think they want us to know what they're up to, and I'm sure they didn't want us to find out about another village. So, for now, our best bet would be to just leave the other village alone. Let's just wait to discover what further developments are in store for us."

My suggestions received agreement.

It was time for our trip to the cave. We gathered up our torches, filled backpacks, and took off. Hopefully we would be back by supper time, but we took some additional supplies just in case.

Cho eagerly embraced our walk to the hill. We had told him about the first cave that we'd discovered, and he was eager to see inside the second.

The walk from Reit was uneventful, and my ankle

was behaving nicely. I had taken the crutches, just in case, but they were currently hanging from my backpack.

At the Hill of Discovery, we first showed Cho the cave that had been closed; it still wasn't easy to find. Then we traipsed around the southernmost part and stood in front of the second cave. There appeared to be some reluctance to enter.

Finally, Stire said, "Let's get these torches lit, and become explorers again." His comment rallied us a little.

The inside of the cave was much larger than I would have imagined. The ceiling was not very high; it appeared to be as high as the top of the two story hill, but the floor seemed to go on forever. In every direction, I could see stacks of rubble, mostly stones and bricks, but well-eroded ones. Frakis immediately took off towards the center of the cave.

"Shouldn't we stick together? Who knows what we'll find?" I was feeling a little nervous, and a little flushed.

"Oh, I think we can stretch out a little, just as long as we keep in view of another torch. Then we can always be near enough to help, if help is needed." Stire looked as eager as Frakis to take off and explore, although he hesitated for a moment after he looked my way.

Cho stuck with me; perhaps he wasn't the adventurous type.

"Where do you want to start, Cho?"

He turned quickly towards me. "Let's go to the left, and hug the wall. That way we can cover the whole room. We don't know how large this cave is; we may need days to discover everything."

"You may be right. But we don't know how long our captivity will last, so let's make the most of today, at least."

Cho and I started walking clockwise around the cave. The first thing we came to was a pile of rubble that might have been a table. The rubble was dark black and shattered, but there were a few long pieces of stone poking out beneath. They could have been table legs. What I found interesting, though, was that the table top had no smaller items on it. All the tables I had ever seen were always piled high, especially in storage rooms.

"Let's keep going," I said to Cho. "I think this must have been a table or something, but I don't see any items of interest around here."

"Agreed; I don't see any artifacts at all."

We walked around a thick pillar that seemed to be supporting the ceiling. The torches of Stire and Frakis flickered in the distance.

Then, before us, there appeared another pile of rubble—but this one looked promising. There were all sorts of small items scattered about. However, the items were a little indistinct in the torch light.

"I think we've found some stone shelves that tumbled down, and some remnants of the items that adorned the shelving," suggested Cho. "Let's get a little closer. Perhaps we can find something useful, or at least an intact relic."

We rummaged around the floor for a while, but we weren't very successful. Most of the non-stone items had disintegrated, and the others were broken.

"Do you have any impression what might have been on these shelves?" I asked Cho.

"These broken bits look like containers. Perhaps this cave was just a storeroom, but a storeroom out in the middle of nowhere doesn't really make much sense. We probably should do more looking around this area. Maybe there's another ancient city to be found."

We started walking, and met up with Stire. He was standing by another pillar, and he had a couple of objects in his hands. "I think I've found a couple of bowls. Almost everything else I've seen has been smashed to bits. At least there appears to be some ventilation. The smoke from the torches is disappearing."

"And there's no musty smell in here," I added. "There must be another opening, so there's a cross draft with…"

A horrendous crash came from a far corner. We carefully picked our way over the rubble, and kept calling for Frakis. We eventually heard a moan. Gradually, we approached the sound; then we saw Frakis lying on the ground.

I rushed towards her and squatted down. "Frakis, talk to me. What happened?"

She coughed for a moment. It sounded like her lungs were full of dust. "I just leaned against a pillar for a moment, and then it collapsed. It turned out not to be as sturdy as I thought it was. Apparently, it was holding up the sky."

I looked upwards and discovered a hole in the ceiling. The sky was as blue as ever, and we now had a little more light in the cave.

Cho started asking a few medical questions.

"My arm is killing me," replied Frakis. She pointed to her left arm with her right hand. She made no attempt to move her left arm.

"It looks to me like you've broken your arm—most likely, a piece of stone fell on it. We need to get you back to the village. The clinic has some splints, and I think you're going to need some pain killers. If it's any consolation, this looks like a nice clean break. We're just going to need to align your arm bones, and tape a splint around it. It should heal in no time."

Cho looked around the cave. "In the meantime, let's get Frakis outside. We can fashion a temporary splint from the first tree we run into. I brought the smaller of the woodcutting tools along with me and, as it turns out, a very necessary roll of tape."

Under much protest from Frakis, Stire picked her up and started the walk back. I was right behind them.

"Wouldn't you rather be carrying Cyn?" Frakis murmured to Stire.

"Why did you say that?"

"Oh, don't growl at me; I'm the invalid. You know what I'm talking about. It's obvious to everyone, except maybe Cyn."

"Actually, Cyn knows how I feel. I told her last night."

"How did she react?"

"I think she's still in shock, and she's uneasy around me. We agreed to leave things as they are for now."

"Right; of course you did. I think I'm going to try and go to sleep for a while. I'm feeling very tired; it must be the pain." Frakis didn't look very convinced at Stire's statement of status quo.

They hadn't realized I was close enough to hear every word they said. Frakis didn't strike me as a gossip, so perhaps Stire's secret was safe. Then, I remembered Janet teasing me about a secret admirer. Apparently I had been the one in the dark!

Frakis woke up momentarily when Cho made her a temporary splint, but then she slept the rest of the way back to our village. We settled her in the clinic, and Cho fixed up her broken arm.

"We'll have someone bring you over some food shortly," I said.

"No rush. I'll probably be sound asleep when dinner arrives; these painkillers are so relaxing." She did sound very sleepy, and her smile was a little thin.

We left her alone and walked across to the cookhouse.

"It seems to be a dangerous profession, being part of the managing committee," commented Cho.

"You have a point. So it's you or Stire next; I've had my turn." And then I thought of Jana, and the strange disappearance of her body. I certainly missed her, but the disappearance was an enigma. What could our abductors possibly want with her body?

Stire and Cho didn't seem inclined to converse much at dinner.

"Ok, guys. Let's go soak in the hot tub. My whole body needs soaking, not just my ankle." They seemed a little reluctant, but they did follow me outside.

I ended up just soaking my foot for a while. Apparently, the entertainment committee had come up with a new game, and Stire and Cho wanted to try it. The game was a bit too strenuous for my ankle, so I just soaked and watched.

The new game appeared to be a bit like volleyball. The entertainment committee had created a removable net using some wire and posts. The object they were throwing about was close to being round. They had covered something light with some big leaves, so it was easy to throw, but they had added some very strange rules. It wasn't like normal volleyball. Only certain people, at particular times, could touch the throwing object. Oh well; I was sure I would understand the rules eventually. I wasn't going to be playing it for a while yet, though.

Suddenly, my reverie was broken by thunder and lightning. It was the strangest bit of weather we had seen—actually, the only piece of weather.

We yelled at everyone to go back to their housing units, and the three of us rushed over to Frakis in the clinic. She was awake from all the commotion.

"What's happening out there?"

"We're having some freak weather. To me, it looks like a thunder storm. You know, loud noises and flashes of light. If it is a thunder storm, it's generally not a good idea to be outside. You can get hit by lightning, and it can be fatal. So we've sent everyone back to their housing units."

"Ok, I've had enough excitement for one day. Are you taking me back home?"

I looked at Stire and Cho. "No, I think it would be a better idea to stay here for the evening. There are lots of beds and blankets. We don't need much else. Who knows? Perhaps the storm will stop quickly."

The storm didn't slow down for a long time. We never made it home.

Chapter 13

A few lightning strikes had marked the ground, but everyone had survived last night's storm.

At the breakfast table, Cho said, "I don't think that storm was natural; It's possible that our abductors were trying to give us a message. In all the days that we have been here, the weather never varied until last night." Cho was looking very unhappy.

"If they were trying to give us a message, then they should send us one in writing, or show themselves to us. Enough of this cloak and dagger stuff." Frakis was unusually cranky this morning; it was probably her arm.

"Watch what you wish for," I said. "Everyone survived the storm, so all is well." However, I really wondered if we had upset our abductors. And, if so, how would they retaliate?

"What are we going to do today?" Stire asked. "We could go back to *Frakis's cave*." Everyone laughed. We had a new name to put on our map.

"I'm up to a walk today, but I really don't want to

go inside that cave. I would be extremely nervous setting foot in there," responded Frakis.

"So let's take off in a direction no one has gone before," Cho suggested. He made a wild gesture, and pointed in a direction. "I don't think anyone has been that way."

So it was agreed, but first we needed to go to the supply box.

* * * *

The crowd was a little anxious as they waited for us to open the box. I must admit, I was too. After it had been opened, some sheets of paper were visible on top. We each picked up the notes written in our own language.

Frakis was the first to speak. "My paper says 'Restore the cameras, or actions will be taken'."

"As does mine," said Stire. My paper was no different.

The crowd started murmuring.

"What are we going to do?" asked Cho.

"Let's get the supplies over to the cookhouse, and we'll have a meeting." Reluctantly, the supplies were ferried over.

The discussion regarding our abductors' ultimatum went on for an hour. Some side topics made the discussion very stimulating.

"Ok, here's a summary of what we have agreed upon. We will take the tape off most of the cameras, but not the ones in our bedrooms. We do need a little privacy," I said. I let the murmuring continue for a moment, and then I raised my hand. "And, as an act of disobedience, we're going to allow room switching. Anyone can stay in any housing unit. It will not be required that each housing unit contains one of each race.

"And now for our most interesting decision: Coupling will now be sanctioned. It's unfair to keep people apart." Brik and Kane were delighted with that decision, but I hadn't decided how I felt. "So let's get to work. We can rearrange any housing units after dinner. In the meantime, I think we have all necessary duties covered for today. If anyone thinks of something we haven't assigned, please let us know." I sat down again with the managing committee.

Jeena waited until after my speech to speak with us.

"How are you feeling?" Frakis asked.

"Oh, I'm still a little tired, so I think it's best I putter in the kitchen today. The Reannone have a very quick recipe for making a slightly fermented fruit beverage, so I thought I'd try making that today."

"Will it be ready for dinner?" I asked.

"Oh yes. Prepare to be surprised!" Jeena strolled happily off into the kitchen area.

"This should be interesting. I didn't know you could make intoxicating beverages that quickly," said Frakis. "Anyway, let's get our packs filled and take off for the day. I'm looking forward to seeing some new countryside."

Our walk took us past the coil. Much to our surprise, it had been destroyed.

"Now I see why we had the storm last night. Our

An Alien Collective – Roxanne Barbour

abductors wanted to destroy the coil so we would stop experimenting with it. Does that mean we're stuck here?" asked Cho.

"I don't think we're stuck here indefinitely. Our abductors can always send us through the supply box, if need be. No, I think they just destroyed the coil to get us to leave it alone, and to send us a message to behave," replied Stire.

"Well, we're not behaving, are we? We're not removing the tape from all cameras, and we're disregarding their order about mixed housing." Cho was angry.

"Let it go, Cho. We need to get their attention, and get some answers about why we're here. We're not going to blindly do whatever they say; that's unreasonable. Surely they realize that. Let's get going." Cho was beginning to annoy me.

We left the coil and continued on our way.

In the direction we travelled, I noticed tall mountains on the horizon. They were perhaps snow-capped, but the distance proved too great for confirmation. The meadows continued to be covered with low lying flowering vegetation, similar to what we had already seen.

One surprise was another grove of fruit trees, but it was quite unlike any we had previously seen. This fruit had an acorn squash shape, but the surface was pink. We decided to pick some on our way back. Hopefully everyone would find them tasty.

On the other side of the grove, we were astonished to discover a huge crater. The crater was so large the opposite side wasn't visible. Rubble covered its floor.

Obviously, the meteor had broken up on impact.

"That's an awfully big crater," I said. "Why isn't there a huge rock sitting in the middle?"

"The meteor was probably wide but thin. Even being thin, it would have made a terrible impact on the planet. It may have even destroyed all life forms," said Stire. That was something to think about; perhaps it was the reason we had only found ruins.

"Let's sit for a while and have some lunch. Perhaps we'll see something interesting in the crater to investigate." I know I needed a rest; our walk had been quite long, and my ankle wasn't completely healed.

We had divvied up some supplies for Frakis, so she didn't have to carry her backpack. She didn't need any further strain on her shoulder or broken arm. After we chose some food, we sat down and took a good long look at the crater.

At first glance, it was overwhelming, but, after a while, a few images began to break through. For me, the predominant image was one of age. In the crater's basin, vegetation was well established. In fact, some of the vegetation looked to be as tall as trees. It would have taken a considerable amount of time for any soil to be created and for air-borne seeds to have taken root.

There were also pools of water. From this distance, they looked quite small, but they were probably much larger than I could imagine.

"I don't think we're going to find much in the basin itself. Everything must have been obliterated when the meteor landed," said Stire. "I think we should be looking around the perimeter of the crater. Perhaps we can find some ruins of a city, or even just a road."

So we dutifully started peering around the circumference. No clues about a civilization were evident to me.

"I don't see anything remarkable," said Frakis.

"No, neither do I. However, I do see a dark spot in the meadow, a little ways to the right. Why don't we walk over there?" I said.

It took us about twenty minutes to arrive at the spot I had pointed out. It was quite unremarkable until Cho discovered that the dark vegetation was actually a plastic-like covering and could be lifted off. There was a lot of tarp to lift, but we were eager to see what was beneath.

What we revealed was a vast area of a concrete-like surface. To make it a little more exciting, one patch of the surface was a slightly different color. We took a closer look, and Stire decided that the small patch could be lifted up. Stire, Cho, and I did the lifting while Frakis watched. What we found was a broad stairway disappearing into the ground.

"Oh, my goodness, whatever can this be?" I was *almost* speechless.

No one ventured a guess.

"This could be a stairway to anything. There could be a storage room down there; there could be another coil; there could be an underground bunker to hide from the meteor…who knows? What I do know is that we need to find a source of light—even if it just is some more torches; I didn't think to bring any with us today," remarked Stire.

"Maybe we should throw something down the stairway. Perhaps there are lights that are automatically triggered by movement," said Frakis.

Nothing happened, though, when we threw a rock down the stairs.

We all had the same urge to explore the stairway, but it wasn't going to happen today. The sunlight only pierced a few feet of the stairway.

"It would be far too dangerous to explore this stairway without some additional light. We don't need any more mangled managing committee. Let's go back to Reit; it's time anyway," I said.

The walk back was uneventful, but I couldn't stop thinking about the massive crater and the stairwell. I would have given almost anything for a camera so we could make some records of our explorations.

The major discussion at dinner seemed to revolve around the housing units' dance; who was moving where? In the end, very little changed. Brik and Kene wanted to be in the same unit, and four Irandi wanted to be together. So it didn't take long to rearrange a few others.

After a long tournament of our new volleyball-like game, *Challenge*, Jeena allowed us to try her new beverage.

"This certainly has an unusual taste," I commented. "I gather, since the fruit is safe for all, this beverage is also?"

An Alien Collective – Roxanne Barbour

"Yes, there's nothing used in the brewing that should affect anyone. So what do you think?"

"I think this is a welcome addition, and I could use another glass of it," I said smiling. "But only one glass; I think there must be some alcohol in it."

"What did you think you would find in a brew?" Jeena poured me another glass of *costs*. Such a strange name they had decided upon.

The evening wound down pleasantly. Frakis had gone home earlier; it had been a long day, and her arm was bothering her.

Stire and I walked over to the supply box. I hoped I would get a brilliant idea about how we should proceed. We leaned against the box, and Stire put his arm around me. I settled into his shoulder. Perhaps it was the *costs* speaking, but it felt so right to be leaning against him.

"Stire, tell me about your family. Do you have any siblings?"

"I have two younger brothers. I'm the oldest; they're still in *first school*. And I have a mother and father."

"Do your parents have careers?" I was curious about the Temman family structure.

"Temmans call it *life-work*, but I think it's the same as career. My parents are both engineers. They met doing their higher education."

"So you're taking after them?"

"A little, I guess. Water preservation is my subject, but I do need to know how to build structures."

"Well, that should prove useful in Reit."

After a few moments of comfortable silence, Stire said, "Cyn, what is your family like?"

I laughed. "Pretty much like yours. I have two siblings also—a brother and a sister, both younger. I live with my parents, and we have lived in the same home since before I was born."

"Do your parents have careers?"

"Widely differing ones: Dad is a chef, and Mom teaches high school, which is like your preschool."

"What does she teach?"

"Mathematics—in the higher grades."

"Another thing in common—you're taking after her."

Stire's right! I hadn't thought of that.

"Cyn, I have a question for you. How do humans show affection? I don't mean family affection; I mean affection between couples."

I turned around and looked at him. He was taking his question quite seriously. "Holding hands and hugging are a couple of ways. Kissing is another. Let me show you."

I decided not to be shy tonight.

My arms went around him, and then I put my lips on his. I didn't find out that evening how Temmans showed affection. We never got around to it.

Chapter 14

We were all at breakfast when an unusual looking alien just appeared in the middle of the dining area. Even though we had survived a frightening relocation from our homes, contact with alien species, new relationships, and much, much more, the appearance of a new being was very unnerving. A very tall humanoid with long curly locks surprised the hell out of me—especially one wearing a cape, and with light blue skin and hair.

"Where is the managing committee?" it asked.

I raised my hand; everyone else just sat there looking stunned. Even though we had begun to adjust to having aliens around constantly, one popping up in the middle of our breakfast apparently freaked everyone out.

"Ah, yes. Now I recognize everyone. I am your guardian; I have been watching over your progress. My question is: why are you doing these acts of rebellion? For example, why are you covering up the cameras, and rearranging the housing? Your group had been cooperating so well."

Everyone looked at me. I didn't know why I was expected to be the one to answer the guardian; there were a lot of people more eloquent than I.

"Because we wanted to get someone's attention! We have many questions, and no one is answering them. So, we strategized to get a response. I guess it worked," I added a little belligerently.

The guardian shook his locks; it was another strange sight to add to my experiences.

"We know that you have many questions—you have asked them often enough." The guardian sounded a little exasperated. "However, the answers are not to be known until this experiment is concluded." The guardian paused for a moment.

Time to get tough!

"So don't answer our questions—just send us home," I demanded.

"We can't do that, either; at least not right now. Please understand that we do not want to harm you."

I interrupted, "The stress of this situation is harmful."

The guardian had obviously come to a conclusion, because he said, "Please stay in your village for the rest of the day. You will find ample provisions in the supply box. I will return this evening with my decision."

"Your decision on what?" I yelled as he disappeared into thin air.

The room burst into many conversations, not the least of which was at our table.

"What do you make of that?" I asked. "I'm more confused than ever. Do you think he's going to send us home?" I looked at Stire after I asked that.

"Unlikely, since it seems that they have bigger plans for us. But for right now, we need to calm everyone. Let me say a few words," said Stire. We all agreed; Stire was well-spoken and attuned to our situation.

"May I have everyone's attention? I know this is frightening and very confusing, but we're going to have to deal with it calmly until we have further information. The rest of our day looks like it's going to be spent in housekeeping, clothes cleaning, cooking, writing notes, etc. Play a few games and just try and relax; the guardian will be back before we know it. Consider today our first holiday. So, let's celebrate the village of Reit." The tension in the room relaxed a little after Stire's speech, and when I started clapping and others joined in, a few smiles began to appear.

"What a turn of events!" said Frakis. "I don't know whether to be excited or scared, or both." She did have a confused look on her face.

"All I know is that I'm starting to feel cranky. Our abductors never answer our questions. Do you really think that will change when the guardian resurfaces later today?" I might have felt cranky, but I was also very scared.

Have we failed some important task?

"Let's just wait and see. We can speculate all we want, but we have no data to help us. Let's just tidy up a bunch of things and have a day of rest," said Stire.

An Alien Collective – Roxanne Barbour

And that's what we did. A little clothes washing, a little tidying of the village, and we were ready for a game.

But first, Stire and I had a picnic lunch in Awakening Square. We needed some time to ourselves.

"What do you think is going to happen?" I asked Stire.

"I have no idea; the guardian gave no clues. I don't even know where to start speculating. I need a starting piece of data before I can imagine the possibilities. All I know is that we have all been stranded here for some reason. That's all I know, and it's nothing," said Stire, with a great deal of frustration in his voice.

I needed to calm him down. "You have to admit, though, that this has been an interesting experience. None of us had ever met aliens before, and now we have just met another one; although this alien seems to be in charge of our lives."

In the future, I needed to think about what I was going to say before I said it. My statement hadn't calmed Stire down, and I had just gotten myself more upset. At least I decided against what I wanted to say next. I didn't think this was the time to tell Stire that meeting each other was at least one good thing to come out of this situation. Who knew what was going to happen to us?

Will we ever see each other again?

So instead I said, "Let's clean up our mess and go back and play a round of that new game. What's it called?"

An Alien Collective – Roxanne Barbour

"I heard Cho call it 'Nober'. I don't know where they got that. And the rules are strange. It almost feels like they change a little every once in a while."

After we gathered our stuff and stood up, I decided that Stire needed a little reassurance—mind you, so did I.

All I said was *sweetheart*, and he gathered me in. We hugged and kissed for a couple of minutes, and then we walked over to the gaming area.

* * * *

I had to agree with Stire; we played a game of Nober and I still wasn't clear on the rules. After one game, I decided I would rather play Ballz. I understood that.

Dinner was a quiet affair. The cooks had gone all-out and made many delicacies. Unfortunately, we couldn't do it justice; we were all anxiously awaiting the guardian's reappearance.

And when he arrived—I was assuming 'he', at this point—he had changed his cape. Now he was in a long and shiny somber black cape that dazzled everyone when he suddenly appeared before us.

"Thanks for being so calm today. I know all of this is, to say the least, uncomfortable." He paused for a moment. "Let me give you a few details. I am part of an advanced race of beings. We do, indeed, have two sexes, in case you were wondering, and I am male. I thought up a name for myself so you would have something to address me by. You may call me *Smut*."

I had to choke back laughter. Stire and Frakis

looked at me like I had lost my mind. Apparently, I wasn't taking this situation seriously enough. I would have to explain my laughter when I got a chance.

"Now, I can't tell you exactly why you are here. That information will come later. In the meantime, be assured that we are very pleased with your handling of these unusual circumstances. You have worked well together, and are beginning to form a community. You have proved to us that you can all get along, even if some mediation is needed occasionally. And this is in no little part due to your managing committee. They have done an excellent job." Smut bowed to us.

We were a little embarrassed, but it was true; we did work well together.

"So, you have all passed our first test. And, no, I won't tell you what these tests are all about. However, I will tell you that you now have seven additional challenges to face. Some of these challenges will be long, and some will be short. Sometimes you may not even realize that you are in a challenge." He looked around at all of us. "Just remember this: we are not pleased with rebellion, but we do understand that intelligent species are not prone to accept everything forced upon them."

Smut sighed. "I probably shouldn't tell you this, but these next seven challenges are important to the future of your races. Work well and work hard. I will see you tomorrow morning after breakfast for your first challenge." And, with that, he suddenly disappeared.

Much discussion ensued; no one rushed outside to play any games.

An Alien Collective – Roxanne Barbour

"So they're putting us on the spot again," I complained. "Controlling our lives, and not telling us why."

"And it doesn't look like we're going to get any answers soon, so we had better step up to the challenges. I really didn't like hearing how we're somehow going to be responsible for the future of our races. And did you notice that Smut said 'future,' not 'futures,' of our races? Do you think that's important?" Stire asked.

"Probably not. Maybe the translator was having difficulty. But I want to know, Cyn, why you were having trouble keeping back laughter at one point," asked Frakis.

"Oh, that's because *smut* means pornographic material in our language. The translation of the guardian's name didn't really seem appropriate, but I guess we're stuck with it."

We all had a good laugh, but I was feeling quite uneasy. This was too much responsibility for young adults.

"Let's go play some Ballz; I need to get my mind on something else. I'm sure I'll be thinking about our situation all night."

After a few rousing games of Ballz, we had a snack and went back to our home. The four of us sat in our lounge for a while.

"I wonder if we'll ever see this village again. Although I miss my family and friends, I have started to become comfortable here. How is everyone else feeling?" I asked.

"I really miss a lot of things. Besides family and

An Alien Collective – Roxanne Barbour

friends, I miss my education and hobbies. I need to be challenged, and not just emotionally," responded Frakis.

Stire and Cho said nothing.

Our gathering broke up when Frakis and Cho went to their rooms. I think they wanted to give Stire and me a little privacy.

Chapter 15

In the morning, the appearance of Smut created quite a commotion. Standing beside him was Jana, with a big smile on her face. I couldn't believe my eyes!

I ran up and hugged her fiercely. "You feel so real," I said to Jana. "Where have you been? We thought you were dead!"

Smut interrupted, "Jana was dead, but the guardians have restored her. We have brought her back here to help you with your quest. Now please sit down, so that I can give you further instructions."

What powers they must have!

I led Jana back to our table. We were absolutely delighted to see her. Jana looked very healthy, and very alive. She was wearing the same clothes she had worn for her service, along with the necklace I had given her.

Smut patiently waited for us to settle down. There was an air of expectation in the dining room. "The guardians do know that your scouts found another village similar to yours. Your first challenge will be to

An Alien Collective – Roxanne Barbour

convince the members of this other village—which doesn't have a name, by the way—to join you on your quest."

I interrupted, "How are we supposed to convince them to join us when we don't know what this is all about?"

Smut said seriously, "Just tell them it's a matter of life and death."

The silence was profound.

"We have been impressed with the governing of this group. So, we would like the managing committee to still be in charge. In fact, your mandate will now include managing the other village as well. You are very adept, and should do well." Smut pulled something from beneath his cape. "Cyn-Tia, this is for you." He walked over to me. "I do believe you have been wishing for a camera to record your activities." Smut handed me a small camera.

"Everyone pay attention, please. We will be going outside now. In Awakening Square you will find a backpack with your name on it. Included in the backpack are a change of clothes, some food and water, and toiletries. There will also be a sleeping mattress and a small communicator. Occasionally, you will be getting further instructions via this communicator. In twenty minutes, we will be leaving the village. In the meantime, go to your housing units, pick up whatever else you wish to take, and then go to Awakening Square to find your pack."

Before the managing committee had a chance to go

outside, Smut came over to our table. He gave us a long look. I couldn't quite interpret his glance, but it looked a little sad. "Unfortunately, Cho, since Jana is back, you cannot continue to be a member of the managing committee. I applaud everyone's attempt to be fair to all races while Jana was gone, but we must go back to the original four."

Cho looked a little stunned.

"Cho, you were a tremendous help to us when Jana was gone. We will most certainly be asking for your advice in the near future," interrupted Stire. Cho seemed to cheer up a bit, and then he left.

"I have a little more information before we begin. After you convince the other village to join you, everyone must walk to the stairway you recently discovered near the crater. It is very close to the other village. Once you arrive at the stairway, further instructions will appear on your communicators. So, pick up whatever else you need and get to Awakening Square. We need to leave soon."

Back at the managing committee's housing unit, we found Jana's belongings that we had stored away when Cho had moved into her room. None of us had acquired much during our stay.

We waited for the stragglers back at Awakening Square.

"By the way, Cyn-Tia, Awakening Square is a nice name," said Smut.

"How many Awakening Squares have you created?" I asked.

An Alien Collective – Roxanne Barbour

Smut just smiled and ignored my question. I really hadn't expected an answer.

"Smut, you do know I think you should change your name. It's not really appropriate," I said.

"So I heard. What do you think about Smale?"

"That'll do fine."

"By the way," said Smale, "Bmit will no longer be with you."

"Why not?" I asked.

"Because he is not actually an Irandi; he is one of our race. We planted him in your village to have a closer ear on the happenings. That is no longer needed."

Really!

I guess Stire was right about someone being a spy.

I decided to take a picture of the gathering crowd. It seemed like an appropriate start to our next adventure.

Chapter 16

Our group at Awakening Square began to disappear in clumps. It was very unnerving seeing people become non-existent. I began to feel a little frightened about the actual experience, but the sensation was anti-climactic. I felt nothing at all—I just reappeared in a different place.

Smale, the guardian, was not in evidence at the new village. I guess all the convincing was going to be up to the managing committee.

We milled around for a moment at the new Awakening Square, and then a few of their inhabitants started walking toward us.

"Who are you? Where are you from?" a tall Irandi asked.

"We are from the village of Reit," answered Stire. "The guardian has sent us here; we need to talk to your managing committee."

"What's a managing committee?" the same Irandi asked.

An Alien Collective – Roxanne Barbour

I glanced at Stire and Frakis. This wasn't the question I had been expecting.

"Who are the people that open your supply box?" asked Stire.

"Oh, you mean our *bosses*. Right now they are in the dining room trying to figure out why we didn't get any supplies today. We're going to get hungry pretty soon. So, we're just hanging around to see if any supplies arrive. The bosses are over there." The Irandi pointed in the direction of their cookhouse.

We suggested to our people that they stay in Awakening Square while we go and talk to this managing committee. During our walk over to the cookhouse, we had a lot to talk about.

"I can't say that this village looks very well organized. I don't see any recreation area, and I certainly don't see any hot tub for the Irandi to do their daily soaking. I wonder how these Irandi are surviving," Jana frowned as she said this.

"Good question; perhaps they built one in another area," I responded. "But the general feeling I get is one of laziness. Their clothes aren't very clean, and there don't seem to be many people engaged in any activities."

"Perhaps it's because they didn't get their supplies today," said Stire.

"Perhaps." I wasn't convinced, though.

At that point, we arrived at the cookhouse. Piles of garbage were stacked against the outside walls, and loud arguing was heard from within. We walked through the cookhouse door, and the arguing stopped.

"Who are you?" demanded a tall, black-skinned human male.

"We're the managing committee from another village, and we've been brought here to give you some information," Stire said.

Our appearance had shocked the second managing committee.

"And what information is that?" he asked.

"First, let me introduce the managing committee from Reit. I am Stire, this is Jana, and Frakis, and Cyn; and you are?"

"Our names aren't important. We run this place, and that's all you need to know."

What a belligerent human, I thought. I didn't know what his problem was; perhaps he was just very scared.

"Very well," continued Stire. "We were visited by the guardian yesterday, and we've all been given our walking orders."

The second committee all started babbling. Finally, they quieted down and their Reannone member spoke. "You'll have to give us some information. For example, who is the guardian, and why do we have to leave?"

"Unfortunately, we don't have all the answers, even though we have asked numerous questions, numerous times. Simply, at least as far as we understand the situation, we were brought here to populate these two villages. This is some kind of experiment by the guardians, but they won't tell us what the experiment is about. And now, they have decided to terminate the village aspect

An Alien Collective – Roxanne Barbour

of the experiment. We're now required to be successful at seven challenges. The first challenge is for our managing committee to recruit your village. Then, the two villages join to overcome the next six challenges."

Stire's explanation is quite clear, I thought.

"Why should we join you? Why don't we just stay here?" asked the human.

"Did you get any supplies today?" responded Stire.

The human shook his head.

"What are you going to live on if you stay here? Have you been butchering meat? Did you find a supply of fruit? How are your gardens doing?" Stire continued.

No responses were forthcoming. To me, they were all looking a little uncomfortable; I didn't think they had been performing their daily duties. I was so glad our scouting crew hadn't contacted them. Stire had been a little harsh, but he had needed to get their attention.

"What will happen, shortly, is that a backpack with supplies will arrive for each person; then you'll be given a few minutes to retrieve anything you don't want to leave behind. Once everyone is organized, we'll set off."

"Where are we going?" asked the reasonable Reannone.

"We'd been out exploring, and found a staircase that went underground. Apparently, it's quite close to your village. The guardian told us the staircase is where the second challenge starts," I answered.

"We haven't decided that we're going," growled the human. "Leave us alone; we have things to discuss."

An Alien Collective – Roxanne Barbour

"Certainly," replied Stire. "But you must realize that any further help or supplies from our abductors will not be available."

We went outside and joined the crowd. Our entire village was at Awakening Square, along with most of this crew. We were bombarded with questions. Stire explained the big picture to the inhabitants of this second village.

"Your managing committee members, I mean bosses, are in discussion right now to decide whether or not to join our group," Frakis added, after Stire had finished his explanations.

"Since you told us that no further supplies will be forthcoming, I'm going back to my housing unit to pick up a few items." The human female that had just spoken glanced towards the cookhouse. "Thanks for letting us know what's going on."

She was followed by the majority of her village. While they were dispersing, three of the second managing committee came out of the cookhouse. They weren't a happy group.

The Reannone spoke, "Hugo Street, the human you met, has decided not to join the trek. He will be staying here by himself unless, of course, others from this village decide to stay."

"I don't think that's going to happen," remarked Stire. "They are all off retrieving their personal items."

"Well, I guess we'd better get busy too."

I watched the three of them walk away. "Don't you think we should try and convince this Hugo guy to join us?"

"Cyn, he appeared to be a very stubborn human," replied Stire. "I don't think any persuasion on our part or yours would be successful."

"Didn't you get the impression Smale wanted us to persuade everyone?"

"He probably did, but it's not reasonable to expect complete agreement in a group this large; there will always be someone that wants to rebel."

Stire is probably right.

Shortly, the group was organized and we started on our walk to the stairway. Our communicators gave us excellent directions.

At first, the two villages were reluctant to talk to each other, but that reluctance soon disappeared. The first groupings I noticed were within species. I guessed they were comparing notes on their experiences.

The Reannone from the managing committee of the second village came up us. "My name is Relu a Kirba. I'm sorry you got such a chilly reception when you arrived; we haven't had a very happy time. Since our committee couldn't get along, the rest of the village suffered. I hope that's behind us now. I can see a little integration going on already." She was of medium Reannone height, but there was something striking about her.

Frakis took pity on her. "It must have been a very difficult situation for you. We have had our share of problems too but, for the most part, everyone was quite reasonable. We're actually quite proud of how we created a community from such disparate beings. Of

An Alien Collective – Roxanne Barbour

course, if we thought we would be living here forever, I'm not sure how it would all work out."

Frakis was right. We were being awfully optimistic about the whole situation. But, for now, I didn't want to consider any other way.

The chatter increased as the huge hole in the ground became visible. I'd forgotten that only the three of us had previously seen the crater. We probably should have warned everyone. We had to walk around a small portion of the crater to reach the stairway. At the entrance to the stairs, there was a sign in all four languages: *Proceed down the stairway.*

Before we started down, I took some pictures of the countryside and everyone milling about. I had been given the camera for a reason.

Chapter 17

No one jumped at the chance, so the managing committee started down the stairway first. Immediately, the stairs were illuminated, and we found an immense stairway—probably ten people wide—descending into the darkness. The lights didn't fail us; they continued to activate and light our way as we tentatively inched forward. It took about five minutes to reach the bottom of the stairway, and there we found an immense cavern.

Immediately before us were some rail cars and a train track going off into the distance. I turned around and saw that the track went both ways.

I was startled by my communicator pinging. We all dove frantically into our backpacks; we had put the communicators away when we started down the stairway.

The first thing I noticed was my name at the top of the flashing screen. *I guess I won't be mixing my communicator up with anyone else's.*

There were only four words, "Get To Next Station".

A hubbub ensued.

"Quiet everyone!" Stire shouted. After a moment, the voices died away. "We need to decide what to do. Obviously, the first step is to figure out how to run this train. Does anyone have any experience with a train like this?" There was no response. "Ok, we need our engineers to take a look at it. We already know who has engineering expertise in our group, but is there anyone else with an engineering background?" A couple of people put up their hands. "Good. All engineers gather over here." While Stire waited for them to arrive, he turned to the three of us and said, "Think of what else we need to do."

Stire is being a little bossy again!

He put a human from our village, named Jackson Tate, in charge of the engineers. They went a little distance away to huddle and discuss strategy. Jackson's arms began waving about but from our distance, I couldn't hear what they were discussing.

When Stire came back, he said, "I have suggested the engineering committee take a lunch break; that's something we all need to do. We should have had a break a while ago."

Stire was right; it had been quite a morning. Everyone sat down and had a rest while we continued to plan.

"I think the only thing we should do while the engineering committee is busy is explore the surrounding areas. We could walk down the tracks in both directions, and also have a crew investigate the stairway. I certainly didn't look at the walls, or anything else for that matter, as I was climbing down here." Frakis said.

"Is it safe to walk down the tracks? Maybe another train will come along." I was concerned about safety.

"It should be fine. If the other trains are the same as this one—and I can't imagine they wouldn't be—then there is plenty of room between the side of the train and the walls," Stire said.

"Ok, then let's limit our exploration to about an hour. Hopefully, the train will be running by then."

We split everyone up into groups and sent them on their way. The managing committee joined in the exploration of the stairway.

The stairway was dark and dingy, even with the lights on. The lights had turned off behind us when we arrived at the well-lit platform. I had been concerned they wouldn't come on again when we started up the stairs, but we lucked out.

We thoroughly scoured both sides of the stairway, and even the stairway itself. Other than a lot of dirt and debris, we only found one item of interest—a hatch. We managed to get the hatch cover off, but there was no illumination.

"I guess seeing inside is out of the question," Frakis said.

"No, it isn't," replied Stire. "I brought along one of our torches and the lighter. This would be an excellent opportunity for using them."

Stire continues to amaze me.

Inside, we discovered a lot of humming machines and a few screens with scrolling alien graphics.

An Alien Collective – Roxanne Barbour

"This must be a control room for the trains," said Stire. "There's probably one at each station. If a train broke down, someone could call for help from here."

"Too bad we don't know their language," Frakis said wryly. We all laughed.

"I don't think we should touch anything; we might get ourselves stranded," I said.

We quickly went down the stairs to the platform. There was quite a crowd; it looked like all of the scouting groups were back.

Jackson approached. "Success! We have started the car that controls the others. It wasn't that difficult. There were some loose wires that were hidden from us; it was almost if someone was being sneaky. Anyway, the train is started, and we have the controls to run it, so we can be off anytime." Jackson was looking quite pleased with himself.

"So everyone worked well together?" asked Frakis.

"Well, not at the beginning." Jackson paused. "Ah, the engineers from the other village were very standoffish; they just stood around and did nothing. But when I gave them something to do, like explore part of the train looking for clues, they perked up and joined in. In the end, I was quite pleased with our results and with the way we worked together."

"Good job, Jackson. We'll make a manager out of you yet," I commented. Jackson just grinned.

"Is everyone here?" Stire asked. He waved Relu over. "Are all your people accounted for?"

"No, we're still missing one. Apparently, one of our

An Alien Collective – Roxanne Barbour

Reannone took off from his exploring group. No one has seen him for a while."

"Which way did he go?"

"He came back in this direction before his group started back."

"Let's just look around the immediate area then. He can't be far."

We organized some teams, but before we could send them out, the idiot surfaced. He was sleeping under the stairs. Our discussions had woken him up.

"Relu?" Stire said.

"I will take care of this. Thank you for your help." And then she motioned the wayward Reannone toward his own managing committee.

"Let's get going. Jackson, you get to steer this beast. Everyone else, get your belongings on board and hold on to your hats; Jackson may need a little practice."

Ok, 'hats' may not have been the best expression to use!

The mood was light as we scrambled into the train cars. There was plenty of room for everyone, and lots of windows for viewing.

The ride was a little rocky at first, but Jackson quickly got the hang of being the train's engineer. He had a slight smirk on his face. Unbelievably, that smirk would hang around for the rest of the day.

Boys and their toys!

The train travelled on a level for a few moments, so there wasn't much to see except walls. Then, suddenly, the train rose and exited above ground into bright sunshine.

I thought our exit from the tunnel would be at the station we were searching for, but there were no facilities in sight. Our pace picked up once we were above ground.

"Jackson, are you getting a little heavy footed?" I asked.

"Actually, I have no control over the speed. I can steer a bit, but it seems to be smoother if I let the train do its own thing. I also have a control that can tell the train to start or stop. However, that's partly an assumption. I figured out the start button, so I'm guessing the other one is for stopping. We shall see." Nonetheless, Jackson was still looking quite pleased. He continued, "This may be a fully automated train system. But since it had been shut down, I'm guessing our challenge was to get it started again. Normally, there may not be any engineers or staff at all."

His statements gave me something to think about.

Our surroundings revealed that we were in an area of the planet previously unseen. The train was travelling quickly through low hills and small lakes. The train seemed to be travelling slightly uphill, so perhaps the lakes were connected by rivers. The lakes glistened with an odd shade of blue.

In the distance, two snow-covered mountains were visible; perhaps they fed the series of lakes. From what little I understood about ecosystems, some seasonal adjustments in the weather would be needed for the snow to melt and feed the water system. During the time we had been here, we had seen no change in the weather. Considering that we had only been here about two weeks, I supposed that wasn't surprising.

The only animal life visible from the train was a couple of herds of grak. They seemed to be common to every area of the planet we had discovered.

After about an hour, I heard a beeping noise coming from Jackson's direction. Stire and I went to investigate.

"The button I thought was the 'stop' button has started to beep," Jackson said. He was looking a little concerned. "Do you think I'm supposed to push it?"

"I don't see how it can hurt. Maybe it's just trying to tell you there's a station up ahead, and asking you if you want to stop," I said.

So Jackson pushed the button. We returned to our seats in anticipation.

"You're an awfully brave person, Cyn," remarked Stire. "The thought of pushing that button and not knowing what it would do made me anxious."

"No, I'm not brave. However, I couldn't think of any other reason for the button to be beeping. Obviously no one else could either, since I didn't hear any objections to my suggestion."

"Well, I think you're brave," said Stire, and he put his arm around me. I definitely needed some comfort at that moment.

Approaching some ruins, the train began to slow and

then, shortly, it stopped in front of the largest building.

Our communicators began to chime.

The notes I received read: "Eat, rest, sleep. In a little while, a meal will be provided for you inside the building. A new challenge will be presented tomorrow morning. Sleep in the train tonight."

And then my communicator pinged again: "CynTia, you have done well today."

Amazingly, that one little statement cheered me up immensely.

We grabbed our backpacks and scampered into the building, or what was left of it. Three of the walls remained, and the roof was still providing protection at one end. We wandered towards that end.

It felt about seven in the evening, and my timepiece confirmed it.

"It looks like we're going to have a later meal than usual tonight. Does it feel a little cooler to anyone?" I asked.

"Yes, it does," said Frakis. "I was thinking about getting my blanket."

"I have a better idea. Why don't we build a fire? There's plenty of material lying about, and Stire has the torch starter."

So, while we waited for dinner, a quite spectacular pile of wood was created.

Shortly after the fire was lit, our food miraculously arrived on tables. Our abductors had outdone themselves again. It was just as well. We were all starving; it had been a long day.

An Alien Collective – Roxanne Barbour

The managing committee found a spot for their picnic.

"What do you think of our two challenges today?" asked Frakis. "Do you think we were successful?"

"I do," replied Stire. "I was given a compliment on my communicator." We all grinned; it turned out we all had received the same message.

"I wonder if anyone else was complimented," I asked.

"Possibly, but let's not pursue it. There are still a lot of disgruntled people—especially from the second village—and we don't want to get them any more irritated," Stire said.

After a very satisfying meal, I discovered I was a little restless. I needed to get my thoughts in order. "I need to go for a walk. Anyone want to join me?"

Stire was the only taker. I think Frakis and Jana would have liked to take a walk too, but I think they were granting us a little privacy.

Stire and I held hands once we were out of view. I started to relax a little; I currently felt very comfortable with Stire. We walked quietly for a while.

Stire broke the silence by saying, "This has been some day, hasn't it? Our lives are so strange right now. I have no idea what's going to happen next."

I answered a tiny part of his uncertainty; I kissed him.

After a moment, he pulled me down onto a flat boulder and said, "Cyn, I would like to rub your head. That is how Temmans give affection." And he proceeded to show me. The texture of the skin on his hands produced a tingling sensation on my scalp. Stire used both hands in what seemed to be a complicated pattern.

I don't know if it was the pattern of motion he was using, or just the feel of his hands on my skin, but I was beginning to experience tingling in other parts of my body.

So, I put my hands on Stire's head and tried to reciprocate.

I took a peek at Stire's face. He had a small smile and his mouth was slightly open. This was not an expression of displeasure. Eventually, he sighed and removed his hands from my head.

"As much as I want to stay here with you, I think we should get back to the others."

I reluctantly agreed and gave him one last kiss.

Chapter 18

Stire and I rejoined the group and, much to our surprise, there was a game of Ballz in progress. Apparently, the entertainment committee had thrown the equipment into their backpacks before we left Reit, and they had retrieved a nice stick from the bonfire material to use as the Abductor.

The inhabitants of the second village took a little while to relax enough to join in the games. If our enslavement lasted much longer, we might need a few more game pieces.

Our little train had plenty of room for everyone. It wasn't long before everyone found their own spot and settled down with their mattresses and blankets. It had been a very long and tiring day. Stire and I found a corner for ourselves, and we quickly fell asleep.

The next morning, while we were freshening up—thank goodness there were washroom facilities on the train—our communicators signaled.

"Pack up your belongings; have breakfast; and in

An Alien Collective – Roxanne Barbour

thirty minutes, go through the blue door."

I don't remember any blue door!

There was a rush to get organized. The tables from last night were again loaded with food, and a blue door had appeared.

The only discussion at breakfast concerned what could possibly lie behind the blue door.

Thirty minutes passed all too quickly. From the body language around us, it appeared that the managing committee would be the first to go through.

"Is everyone ready?" I asked. "We seem to be the vanguard again."

Before anyone could respond, our communicators beeped.

"In the quickest possible time, everyone must reach the RED DOOR."

The room began to buzz.

"This is awfully mysterious," commented Frakis. "I guess it's our next challenge, but they could have given us a little more information."

"Let's just do it," I said. "We won't be enlightened standing around here."

We picked up our backpacks and walked towards the blue door. After a few seconds of hesitation, I opened it. I was immediately greeted with a wall of fog.

"Ok, here's goes nothing," I said as I pushed through the fog.

Much to my surprise, I exited into a large sandy open area that was surrounded by tall shrubs. After the last person joined us, the fog and blue door disappeared.

An Alien Collective – Roxanne Barbour

"I don't see any red door," said Frakis.

"It looks like we're going to have to search for it. And, by the number of paths leading away from here, I bet this is one very big maze. We're going to need to explore all the paths to find the red door. There's no way we could get lucky enough just going down one path," I said.

"You're right. We'll have to split up and investigate. A method of communicating with each other would be nice," Stire added.

Jack cleared his throat. "Actually, we can talk to each other through these communicators. Well, talk is not the right word, though. Janet and I figured out how to send written messages to each other, Cyn, I'm sending you a message now."

My communicator pinged, and a message appeared. *"Isn't this fun?"* And the top of my screen said it was from Jack.

"That was convincing," I said. "So, now we need someone to be the central contact. Jack, I do believe you have been elected, since you're our historian."

The look on Jack's face confirmed the delight I knew he would feel.

"That's fine, but I'll need someone to help me. I want to draw a map of the maze here in the sand. If we can get one that's fairly accurate, then when a group finds the red door, we can determine the quickest path for the other groups to rendezvous. After all, we were told to do this as quickly as possible."

"I can think of no better plan, Jack," Stire said.

"Let's figure out how many paths there are, and get exploring groups organized."

There were seven paths to take. Since three people were staying behind with Jack, that made eight or nine people per exploring group. For this challenge, the managing committee decided to split up.

"Don't forget, you can keep in touch with me personally," suggested Stire, as we parted.

That's so sweet!

Before my group left, I went over to Jack and his crew. They had already started on their map in the sand. They had drawn the open area in the middle, and used some stones to indicate the start of each path. They were busy gathering up twigs and leaves to start indicating the twists and turns they knew they would be recording.

"You guys are doing an amazing job, and we haven't even left yet."

Jack just grinned. "I love maps, and this is going to the most important one so far. You'd better get going; our abductors have put us on a time limit."

"Yes, boss," I said, and ran over to my group. "Ok, let's go."

All paths appeared to start the same. It would be interesting to compare notes at the end of this challenge.

There were eight in our group, and we were the last to take off.

"Let's move quickly," I said.

We set off at a very brisk walk down our path. The shrubs were about ten feet tall, but the sky was still visible. After a two minute walk, we took a sharp turn to the right. At that point, we needed to communicate with Jack. He was creating his map by paces. We knew that everyone's pace was not the same, but it was a close enough estimate. Each group had two people counting their paces, in case someone got confused. I sent the relevant information to Jack, and we continued on our way.

The path was wide enough for two, so I was walking alongside Simner, one of the two scouts that had found the second village.

"Ah, Cyn, I know this is none of my business, but you and Stire seem to be getting close."

"Yes, we are. It's all a little strange, though."

"I can only imagine. Do you think your relationship with Stire is wise? We have no idea what's going to happen."

"No, it's probably not wise, but we didn't go looking for this complication. Perhaps, when we have some time, you and I can talk about what life is like for a female Temman."

Before Simner had a chance to answer, we came to an abrupt halt. Our path diverged in two directions. Our big dilemma was which path to choose.

I sent Jack a message with the details of how many paces we had walked, and our current situation.

After a couple of minutes, I received a message. "Continue on the left path. I'm pretty sure I know where the other one goes."

We followed his directions, and then we arrived at

An Alien Collective – Roxanne Barbour

a point where our path took, once again, another sharp right. The builders had a craze for right angles.

Our path continued for only a short time before it took a sharp left. And then, in a few moments, another sharp left.

Now the path seemed to continue for a long time in a straight line. The shrubs were changing a little as we went along. They became a foot or two shorter, and they continued to be dark green, but of a different shade.

The size of the maze overwhelmed any previous maze I had ever experienced. Of course, our abductors were capable of many things; who knew what else we were going to experience.

Shortly after crossing another path, we turned left. The shrubs were now an additional foot shorter and their hue was turning blacker. I decided that might be some information that Jack could use on his map. So I tried to recall my impressions of the shrubbery on our route, and sent him a note.

One last turn left, and our path abruptly ended. We were surrounded by shrubs; I didn't know what to think.

Is this a dead end?

Simner spoke. "The shrubs at the end of the path are a little different; let's look behind them."

It wasn't an easy task; they were quite prickly. After a portion of the shrubs were torn away, some red appeared. That glimpse of red galvanized our group into removing the rest of the shrubs. A red door appeared before our eyes, and there was a lot of cheering. I sent Jack a message detailing our success.

"Let's go," cried someone.

"We can't," I replied. "We're supposed to go through the door together. Jack will now direct everyone our way. Let's sit down and have a rest; I know I could use something to drink."

Over the next thirty minutes, groups began trickling in. It was then that I got an urgent message from Jack.

"One of the groups is lost. I think they forgot to give me one of their directional updates because I have them going in the wrong direction. My best guess is that they are close to your position. They're sitting down, so they don't get any further away."

I thought furiously. Three paths converged at my location.

"Ok, I need six of the fastest runners we have. We need to find a lost team."

I got the teams of two organized and sent them out. "Keep in touch, and go as fast as you can. We're running out of time." I had not anticipated a glitch like this.

I waited anxiously; Stire was in the lost group. I sent a message to Jack to get his team to the red door.

Thankfully, it was only fifteen minutes before the group was found. Jack and his group arrived at the same time as the lost group.

After a brief moment of reunion, we took a deep breath and opened the red door.

Chapter 19

After going through the red door, we once again encountered a wall of fog, but, on the other side, delights awaited us. There was a lake with a picnic area, and tables loaded with food and drink. The horde quickly descended on the feast.

"Our abductors may be bombarding us with challenges, but at least they are keeping us well fed! Although, I do miss our meals back at the village. Do you think we'll ever see Rcit again?" I said.

"Very unlikely," said Stire. "We're being tested for some reason. If we were meant to stay indefinitely in Reit, I'm sure we would have met our challenges there."

Stire's logic was somewhat convincing.

Towels were stacked on one of the tables, and that gave me an idea.

"I'm going for a soak in the lake. I need to wash off some of this grime." I took my clothes off, except for my underwear, and dashed into the lake. It was delight-

An Alien Collective – Roxanne Barbour

fully warm. Apparently I started a stampede; the whole crew ended up in the lake. Some just went in to wash up, but a few water fights broke out amongst others. The Irandi were particularly happy having a soak.

After I dried off and changed, I felt refreshed. Maybe there was time to take a nap; the recent days had been strenuous. However, our communicators pinged shortly, and we had a new message.

"Well done on your previous challenge. You will find a red light on the other side of the lake. Make your way there before three hours have passed."

A red light was indeed visible on the opposite lakeshore, although no one remembered seeing it before we got the message. We turned around from looking across the lake and discovered a huge stack of items had materialized behind us. There was an immense pile of what looked like foam, planks, and ropes.

"How are we going to get everyone across the lake in three hours?" Frakis asked.

"Perhaps we could walk around the lake," I said.

"I don't think so. Take a careful look at the lake; I think we're at the narrowest spot. The lake goes off in the distance both to the right and left of us," Stire replied. "I believe it would take a lot more than three hours to go around."

Jackson interjected, "From the looks of that pile, I think we're meant to make rafts and personal flotation devices. I think I even saw some poles. I'm guessing the lake isn't very deep."

"Interesting thoughts," replied Stire. "We'll send

someone out to determine how deep the lake is. Let's go over to the pile and see what's there."

The pile was quite immense, and there were a lot of foam blocks.

"Jackson, can you get a crew together and start on the rafts?" Jackson nodded and walked away towards some of the other engineers.

"Some of this material looks just right for personal flotation devices. We could probably paddle with our hands, but perhaps we could fashion something for paddling. However, you must understand that we Temmans are not that comfortable around large bodies of water. Our planet has very little water, so we have limited experience with something like a lake—especially if we're supposed to get across it. Temmans will be the most comfortable on a raft as opposed to a small flotation device. We don't actually know how to swim."

Stire was almost babbling; he was more than a little anxious about the water. I guessed cleaning up in a lake was a little different than floating on a large body of water.

Our swimmer came back at that moment. He had only gone a little ways across. His opinion was that the lake was shallow, so poles should work very well.

We worked as quickly as possible, but it still took an hour to get everyone provided with some sort of flotation device. We had quite an assortment of both individual floaters and rafts. The managing committee was together on a raft, since we wanted to keep Stire company.

An Alien Collective – Roxanne Barbour

The flotilla started off with only a couple of hiccups. A few individuals raced off ahead, but most of us tried to stick together.

The afternoon was lovely. Most of the days on this planet had been acceptable; the only dark spot I could remember was the thunder storm.

We took turns poling the raft along. While Stire and I poled, Frakis and Jana sat and had a quiet chat, and then we reversed our positions. Stire and I hung our legs off the back of the raft and silently reflected about our situation—or at least I did.

Frakis shouted, "Everyone hang on, there's a huge wave coming our way! Pass the message on!" I couldn't believe it; up until now, the lake had been entirely placid. Frakis had seen the wave before anyone else because our raft was on the outer edge of the flotilla.

The wave hit with a tremendous force. Stire and I went flying off and into the lake. Stire struggled desperately to keep his head above water, so I grabbed him. He was such a limp weight; he was no help at all.

"Frakis, Jana, I need some help. I can't handle Stire on my own."

Jana jumped into the water while Frakis held onto the poles and tried to steer the raft towards us. Between Jana and me, we could barely hold Stire above water; he was such a dead weight. It took the three of us to haul him onto the raft. Eventually, he came around, coughing and sputtering.

"I really don't like bodies of water," Stire gasped. "Is everyone else all right?"

An Alien Collective – Roxanne Barbour

We hadn't even thought of the others as we were resuscitating Stire.

We called to the others. Everyone had survived, but there were quite a few shaken people, especially Temmans.

Jackson had some information. It appeared that one of the rafts had lost its poles during the wave.

"My raft and another are going to tow the disabled one," said Jackson. "I had brought along some ropes, in case we needed them, so it'll work out fine."

Good planning.

We regrouped and started again. The word was passed that time was getting tight.

"Do you think that wave was natural?" I asked Jana and Frakis. Stire was lying down and resting; actually, I thought he had fallen asleep. Almost drowning seemed to make one a little tired.

Frakis replied, "No, I don't. It was just a little too convenient that the wave appeared when we were in the middle of the lake. I think our captors were adding a little spice to our lives. Perhaps we've been solving the challenges a little too easily."

"Well, we still have three left. Let's hope that they don't get too creative in the future."

Getting to the landing site was a little anti-climactic. We did make it in time, but with only about five minutes to spare.

"We barely made that finish line," I commented to Frakis. "Hopefully the future challenges will be a little easier."

An Alien Collective – Roxanne Barbour

"I'll drink to that," replied Frakis.
Then our communicators pinged again.
"Dinner will be served in one hour."

Chapter 20

It was nice of our abductors to let us know we were going to eat again, but I was getting frustrated. The only thing we knew was that only three challenges remained.

I decided that a little paddle in the lake would calm me down. I really didn't need another dip, as I'd already experienced two today—one voluntary and one not. However, a little floating would be very relaxing and, hopefully, I could shut my mind off for a little while.

"What are you doing in there?" asked Stire, after I had been in the water for a few moments.

"Just floating."

"Why would you want to float?"

"It's very relaxing. I've had a stressful day. Why don't you come in too?"

"I don't know how to float, remember?"

Oh, I remember!

"Just go into the shallow part and sit down. Find a spot where the water is up to your shoulders when you sit. That should be quite relaxing for you."

An Alien Collective – Roxanne Barbour

Slowly, Stire approached the water. Gradually, he walked out to where the water was just below his waist. Then he gingerly sat down. I didn't go near him during this time; he had a *don't fuss over me* look on his face.

I watched him slowly relax.

"This is not so bad. Eventually, I might even like being in water over my head." Stire smiled.

I took a chance. "Would you like me to help you float?"

He looked at me speculatively. "I guess so."

I stood up and gestured to Jana. "Will you help me get Stire to float?"

"Oh, no problem." Irandi did love their water.

We slowly had Stire lean back as we lifted his abdomen.

"Now, just relax. You can't float if you tense up. Breathe slowly; lean your head back. Now spread your arms and legs out. And relax a little more."

Slowly, Stire began to relax. After a few moments, I gave Jana a look. As unobtrusively as we could, we took our hands from Stire's body.

In a moment, Stire said, "You're right; this is very relaxing."

"Could you stay here all day?"

"Well, maybe not all day, but for a little while longer, perhaps."

"Good, because Jana and I are going to get dressed. If you open your eyes, you can see our hands. You're on your own."

In horror, Stire began to thrash about, and then he

sank. We pulled him up out of the water.

Jana and I were laughing helplessly. Stire chased us for a little while, and then we all collapsed on the ground consumed with laughter. Even Stire could see the humor in the situation.

* * * *

Again, our abductors provided a wonderful dinner. By this time, we were all starving; it had been a long day.

"I wonder what's happening to our gardens?" asked Frakis. "They were starting to come along very nicely." Frakis sighed; she had enjoyed working with the plants.

"How is your arm feeling?" I asked.

"Actually, it's not bad at all. I need to keep the splint on, but it doesn't hurt very much."

We heard a thrashing in the woods. Then Hugo Street, who had stayed behind at the second village, appeared.

He looked a little disheveled, and he tried hard not to appear happy to see us. I wasn't particularly happy to see him.

"How did you find us?" asked Stire.

"A communicator and backpack were left for me. It wasn't difficult to figure out your position from clues on the communicator. Actually, if you know what buttons to push you can find a map of the planet, too."

"Show me," demanded Stire.

It was true; the map wasn't difficult to find. We just hadn't had any time lately to do anything except survive.

An Alien Collective — Roxanne Barbour

"Help yourself to some food," I said grudgingly. Hugo looked very hungry.

Hugo walked away, and I turned to the others. "I don't like this. We've had to endure all these challenges. Why does Hugo get to avoid them?"

"Be a little gracious, Cyn. I agree he should have been with us for the challenges, but that's the past. He'll be joining us for the last challenges." Frakis gave me a look that I took as reproachful.

I don't remember ever getting any graciousness from Hugo.

Our communicators pinged again.

"You will shortly be receiving a stack of material. Please show us your artistic and musical abilities."

I was astonished. Why would our abductors want to know about our art and music? The only thought that came to mind was that perhaps they wanted to see the differences between our cultures.

A huge stack of items appeared behind the food tables. A few people rushed over immediately; the rest of us gradually wandered that way. Some reluctance was evident; I had a feeling a lot of people had never explored their artistic side. I had found out over the past few days just how technologically minded a good number of us were.

I watched the others for a while. A few people were starting to make what looked like drums. Stire was one of them.

"What are you making?" I asked him.

"On our planet, we call it a *rack*. You pound on it

with your hands and keep the rhythm for musical performances. I do enjoy racking; it's good exercise, and it relaxes me."

"I can see that." Stire had a huge grin on his face.

An option popped into my mind. "I'll leave you to it. I'm looking for some paint and canvasses."

I searched around the stack and found some paints. There were small tubes and large tins of various colors, and some brushes. A number of canvasses were stacked nearby.

"Cyn, are you going to paint?" someone asked.

I turned around and there were Jeena and Janet. "That's the idea."

We discussed everyone's ideas. My idea was to create a large mural depicting our stay on this planet, all the wonders we had seen, and our strange experiences.

I found a roll of what looked similar to canvass and some boards, and convinced Jackson to build us a big canvass to paint on. He happily went to work.

So Jeena, Janet, and I proceeded to paint a very large mural. It took us a couple of hours, but we were pleased with our result.

Frakis came over and chatted. "This is amazing. It's like a visual history of what has happened to us. I don't think you guys have missed anything; you've even got a little picture of Jackson and crew fixing the train."

"Janet did that," I replied. "And I think it's a remarkable likeness of Jackson. I was better at painting the scenery, so Jeena and Janet let me do that." We all

An Alien Collective – Roxanne Barbour

laughed. It had been quite a cooperative effort, and much fun.

"If you guys are finished, let's walk around and see what else has been created."

We slowly strolled through our little encampment, and saw some wondrous things. However, some of the creations were inexplicable to me. For example, someone had found some wire and putty-like material and was making a sculpture; that part I understood. I just didn't have a clue what the sculpture was meant to represent.

"Frakis, do you know what that sculpture is about?" I asked, since the artist was a Reannone.

"I'm assuming it's a sculpture to one of our gods. Our gods are each represented by a shape, so you see sculptures all over the place, at home, having similar outlines. I'm not sure what this one is supposed to represent. It's obviously in its earliest stages." I decided she was trying to tell me it wasn't very good.

"Frakis, what did you make?" I asked.

"Oh, I made a *mire*," she answered. "I found some lengths of metal, and I got Jackson to help me put it together. Let's go over there, I'll show you." Frakis pointed in Stire's direction, so we wandered that way.

The instrument that Frakis pointed to reminded me of something, and then it came to me. The mire was very similar to a xylophone—very ingenious.

She sat down beside Stire, and a couple of other drummers, and they began to improvise. It was quite astonishing; I would never have been able to be so creative.

Jana was standing beside me and listening, so I suggested to her, "Let's wander around and see some other artistic endeavors."

In a dark corner, we came upon Hugo Street, sitting alone.

"Hugo, what have you been involved in?" asked Jana.

"Nothing; this is a complete waste of time. I refuse to cooperate with any of the demands we are receiving; that's why I refused to go along on the trek."

"Then why are you here? Why did you join us?" Jana asked.

"Because I ran out of food. Now, leave me alone." Hugo turned his back to us.

"We need to have a meeting about this," I said to Jana, loudly enough that Hugo couldn't help but hear. "We are all in this together, and we must all do our parts, or there will be consequences." Jana nodded, but she had a very bleak look on her face.

We quickly walked back to Stire and Frakis. However, when we got there, a concert was in progress. A few additional musical instruments had been constructed, and the band was accompanying a lovely Irandi singer. She had an amazing voice. After she sang a couple of songs and stopped for a moment's rest, our communicators pinged.

What now?

"A nice set of accomplishments. A snack and some beverages, including fermented ones, will soon be arriving. All items can be tolerated by everyone. Shortly, tents will show up. Get a good rest; tomorrow will be a long day."

We picked up some snacks and beverages and wandered over to admire the large mural I had helped paint.

"I don't think your painting missed much of our journey," commented Stire. "Although you might have to start another mural if our experience continues much longer."

"According to my count," said Frakis, "we have only two challenges left."

We thought about that for a moment. Jana spoke up and relayed our encounter with Hugo to Stire and Frakis.

"What should we do about him?" I asked.

"I really don't want to have him exiled; I think that's a little harsh," Stire said.

"Yes, but he should participate. He's shirking his duty and is just along for the food."

"Let's leave the problem of Hugo until tomorrow. Perhaps he'll participate in the last two challenges, and then our problem will be solved. You may have scared him into cooperating when you spoke with him earlier," Stire said.

"Let's go get some more beverages, and speculate on what tomorrow might bring." Frakis said.

That was the best idea I had heard all day.

Chapter 21

"Last night was very enjoyable," said Frakis. "I had missed having some musical entertainment. The amount of creative genius in our group is unbelievable."

"Yes, we're all brilliant," said Jana. "Even Cyn and her painting." We all laughed.

"I knew there was a reason they only let me paint the background." I paused. "So what's going to happen today? There are only two challenges left."

Before anyone had a chance to speculate, our communicators pinged.

"Finish your breakfasts, and gather up your packs. Follow the arrows to the next meadow. All sixty-four people must participate in this challenge. At the meadow, create groups of eight—two from each race. You will find four obstacle courses; you must participate in all. Each end of an obstacle course is a starting point. Good luck."

I looked around to find the arrows. They had suddenly appeared, and were pretty obvious. Apparently there was a meadow past the grove of trees situated on one side of our campsite.

"Let's put together a team of the two managing committees. That way we can get Hugo involved, and not hiding out," suggested Frakis.

Stire went to find the other managing committee, while the rest of us packed up our bags and his. The guardians had included bottled water and snacks with breakfast.

There was a lot of milling about, but no firm groups were being formed.

"We need to get this organized," I said to Jana and Frakis. "Let's go our separate ways and get groups created before we set off for the meadow."

At the meadow, the start of each obstacle course was obvious. Much to my surprise, everyone was sitting down in their groups and awaiting the word of the managing committee.

"We'd better get everyone started," said Stire. "Let's get four groups started at this end, and then lead the rest to the other side of the courses."

After the other groups were on their way, the managing committees started on the last obstacle course. Approaching the first obstacle, our communicators pinged.

"Navigate over the log."

"I think our communicators are picking up a signal from the obstacle," said Stire.

"That would only make sense, as we are all experiencing different obstacles at the same time," added

Frakis. "It would be pretty difficult to keep track of every individual."

I took a good look at the first obstacle. It was a log supported at Frakis's chest height, and it looked very slippery.

I came up to the obstacle last. I couldn't figure out how to get over it. I was shorter than Frakis, and I could barely reach the log. While I was contemplating my options, I felt myself being lifted up. Stire had come up behind me and given me a boost.

"You need to grow a little," he said, trying to contain his laughter.

On the other side, I gave him a hug. I sure hoped my height was not going to be a disadvantage today.

The next obstacle was a ladder at a forty-five degree angle. We were to climb up one side, and then down the other. I had never climbed down the backside of a ladder, and it was quite a novel experience. For me, the sensation was like hanging upside down.

For the third obstacle of this course, we had to weave over and under some logs that had been supported about three feet off the ground. Everyone was moaning about their backs when we finished.

"Did you notice these obstacles have all been inscribed with the number eight? It looks like we'll be going through groups of obstacles. I wonder what our abductors are trying to find out."

No one had an answer for Frakis.

The final obstacle in the eight series was a series of stumps that we had to jump along. This was particularly difficult for Stire, since he didn't have the daintiest of feet.

"The next obstacle is a nine. Let's stop for a moment and have some water. This is really thirsty exercise." I was in need of a rest, too.

Before we started again, Hugo came up to us and announced, "I'm not doing this anymore. I'm going back to the campsite."

"No, you are not," replied Stire. "You will continue along the obstacles with the rest of us."

"Make me!" Hugo looked a little flushed.

"Yes, I could tie you up and make you. But it would be better if you came along of your own volition. After all, the reputation of humans is at stake." Stire brandished a length of rope. I had no idea where he had gotten that. Reluctantly, Hugo agreed to continue.

"Ok, everyone, we'd better get going. We're not even through the first obstacle course yet." Frakis did know how to cut to the chase.

The first obstacle labeled nine was not too bad. We had to walk up one inclined log, and then down another.

Playing Tarzan was another matter. We had to climb up one ladder to another ladder that was held up by an additional ladder. We were supposed to grasp one rung of this suspended ladder and hang down. Then we needed to traverse the rest of the length of the ladder by releasing one hand at a time and swinging forward and grasping the next rung, until we reached the end rung, and then climb down the third ladder.

This exercise was particularly difficult for the

An Alien Collective – Roxanne Barbour

Reannone. Evidently, their antennae objected when their feet weren't planted firmly on the ground. So Stire volunteered to walk underneath them and put his hands on the soles of their feet—he was the only one tall enough. Thankfully, their antennae bought into the illusion. This was one of the strangest things I had ever seen, so I continued to take lots of pictures.

Our next obstacle was a belly crawl. We hurried through that, since we had the impression we were getting behind. The only discomfort I encountered was a lot of sawdust in my mouth and eyes.

The last obstacle in nine proved to be a challenge for the Irandi in our group. The challenge was an inverted rope descent. Each of us needed to climb a ladder, and then descend to the ground upside down, just holding on to the ropes with our feet and hands. The Irandi didn't like to be upside down. They did the challenge, but the rest of us were holding our breath as they did so; we couldn't figure out any way to help them. Finally we were at the end of the first obstacle course. We collapsed on the ground.

"We're only a quarter of the way through. How are we going to last through the remainder?" I was quite sweaty; that rope descent had done me in.

"Eat something; you'll feel better in a moment," said Frakis. "We've probably done the hardest obstacle course first." Frakis was ever the optimist.

We were on the other side of the meadow—at the starting point for the first four groups. There were a couple of other groups also resting on the ground. It was true; they weren't looking nearly as exhausted as we were.

After a few moments, Stire hustled us along.

The first obstacle of the second course was six logs we had to vault over. Thank goodness, they weren't too high.

Then we encountered a series of logs suspended like swings. We needed to get over all five of them; it wasn't as easy as it sounded. It was easier to get over a log that was fixed and not swinging wildly. We soon learned to hold the log for each other.

The last obstacle in set ten was interesting. We needed to take a run, then grab a rope, and swing ourselves onto the top of a low wall that was quite wide.

After I stepped off the wall, I heard a scream behind me; Frakis had fallen off the wall. I rushed over to her.

"I'm ok. It's just this arm of mine—I can't hold onto anything very well since I broke it. And now I've landed on it again; I don't think I've made it any more broken though." She did have a pained expression on her face, but I could see she was desperately trying to smile.

The next three obstacles were visible just ahead of us. There was no way that Frakis was going to be able to do them; they all involved climbing or crawling.

"You need to rest these next ones out," I said to her. "You can't climb or crawl with a broken arm. I don't know why we let you do some of these other ones."

Hugo interrupted, "But everyone has to do them, you said."

"Within reason. When you break your arm, we'll let you out of some of them," Stire responded.

Obviously, Hugo considered Stire's words a threat. I didn't think Stire meant to break Hugo's arm, but it wouldn't hurt for Hugo to think so.

"Let's go," I said, breaking their staring match.

The first obstacle, labeled eleven, was a belly scraper. It had a number of logs suspended above ground. We first stepped up onto a lower log and then lay on our stomachs and crawled along until the logs came to an end. My stomach had never felt so flat.

The next obstacle seemed a little tame. We climbed up a ladder to a platform and then jumped to the ground. Stire caught me as I approached the ground.

"That looked a little high for you," he just said. It was nice to be in his arms. We hadn't had much time alone lately, so I kissed him.

I noticed Hugo looking at us speculatively.

The last obstacle in eleven was quite complicated. We had to climb a rope so we could clamber onto a platform, walk across some slippery logs, climb higher up another ladder and then climb down to the ground using a cargo net suspended on the opposite side. We were very careful, and took our time. We did have a little slippage on the cargo net but, in the end, all was well.

There was another group milling about when we emerged from our second obstacle course.

An Alien Collective – Roxanne Barbour

"We saw you coming through, so we decided to wait for a moment before we started this course," said Jackson. "How have the courses been?"

"Very demanding," Stire answered. "How about yours?"

"Not so bad. Just a bit of exercise and such. Lots of hurdles and foot work."

"See, I knew our group went through the most demanding obstacles first," said Frakis. I hoped she was right, because I was beginning to fade.

All too soon, we started the third obstacle course. It was obvious we were going to be doing a lot of crawling.

Frakis offered to move our backpacks along from obstacle to obstacle while we crawled through them. There was no way she was going to be able to participate with a broken arm.

There were three obstacles—a large pipe to crawl through, a series of low rails to crawl under, and wire tied to posts to navigate beneath. The only stipulation was that we had to do it blindfolded. Frakis helped us by standing at the end of each obstacle to let us know when we were through.

As I was crawling through the tunnel, I could hear someone yelling. I quickly slithered through and took my blindfold off.

Hugo was yelling, "Get me out of here! I'm trapped." He wasn't trapped, but he had become hooked on the wire obstacle.

I ran over. "Take your blindfold off," I instructed. "Then take some deep breaths. You're not trapped;

you've just become caught in the wire. Here, let me unhook you." After I released him, he calmed down a little. "Take some more breaths, and then start crawling. You're almost at the end."

The crawling exercises didn't take long. Three more obstacles appeared before us. Apparently, we needed to practice our footwork.

"It looks like you're back in the group," I said to Frakis. "It's time you got a little exercise again."

"Yes, I have been feeling quite slovenly." She always did have a sense of humor.

We made short work of these obstacles. Two of the obstacles were mazes to maneuver about, and the third was crisscrossing logs that we had to step through. They took quite a bit of concentration, but were quickly completed.

It was time for another rest; three courses down and one to go.

"I'm glad there's only one course left," said Frakis. "I'm getting tired."

"I think we've done quite well, though," Stire added. "These have not been trivial tests of our stamina."

"It sure looks like our abductors have been trying to see how physically fit we are," I said.

"Yes, but why?" questioned Frakis. No one had an answer.

"Let's just get this last course done. I need a long rest," I said.

The first obstacle was a series of elevated planks that we had to walk along. To make them a little more difficult, there were twists and turns in how the planks were put together. This was a little difficult for Frakis. Balancing with only one arm proved to be a challenge for her.

Then we encountered a series of ditches to jump over. Stire had no problem, but a couple of us did, as our legs were shorter.

Our final task was vaulting over some low fences and walls. They weren't that difficult, but our energy supply was very low.

We sat in the meadow at the start of the obstacle courses and waited for the other groups to appear. As they finished, we sent them back to camp, so they could have a rest or a swim while we waited to find out what was next in our lives.

Shortly, we also traipsed back. I was feeling so sweaty that I did have a short swim. Stire felt brave enough to at least wash himself off in the lake.

While I was drying myself off, lunch arrived without any notice, and that was very unusual. We fell ravenously on the food.

While we ate, we compared notes with other groups. Everyone had managed to make it through the obstacles, but there had been some tough times.

"You know, I think we all need a nap. It must have been a strenuous morning for everyone. Look at that group over there;" said Jana, "they're all falling asleep."

"I must admit to being very sleepy myself. I can't keep my eyes open," I said, with a yawn.

The last thing I heard was Stire saying, "Something's wrong…"

Chapter 22

I was having the most wonderful of dreams, and then I woke up. Or, at least, I thought I woke up. I was in a very dark room, and nothing was visible. Out of the darkness, I heard a voice say, "With what types of people do you enjoy spending time?"

What kind of question is that?

Was one of our abductors asking the question? I didn't know what to think.

Again I was asked, "With what types of people do you enjoy spending time?"

I decided to go along—for now. "I like people that are intelligent and have a sense of humor. I like open-minded, reflective personalities. And I really like people who enjoy reading and writing, and doing artsy stuff."

"Why do you enjoy these specific qualities?"

"I guess I really like people that think about things; who consider how circumstances impact the world and their own lives. As for artistic people, I don't have much talent in those areas, but I would like to be able to accomplish some of the things they do. Oh, and I like people that play games; I like a little competition."

"Do you seek out people that are similar to you, or different?"

What is with all these questions?

"I do like people that have similar interests, but I also need to be with people that are different. That's why, on one level, I'm finding this situation we're in very stimulating. But, on the other hand, I certainly do miss my family and friends."

That got me to thinking about home. We'd been so busy the last few days just trying to cope that I had spent very little time reminding myself how lonely I was. Having Stire, Frakis, and Jana around helped alleviate some of my loneliness.

Are they going through the same questioning I am?

"What are two of the group activities you enjoy?"

That question made me think for a moment. "I guess it would be sharing a meal, and playing a game." We needed to get more games organized.

How delusional is that! I had no idea what was going to happen to me, or anyone else, for that matter. I didn't even know where the other sixty-three were at this moment.

"What types of activities did you enjoy as a younger person?"

Crazy questions!

"I enjoyed solving puzzles and building models. Reading was also a pleasure, and it still is, although perhaps not currently. And I loved learning new things at school." Annoyance was starting to creep into my voice.

"What career are you looking forward to?"

That was easy. "Something to do with mathematics and computers."

"What is the biggest attitudinal change you would like to make when dealing with others?"

This was definitely a change of subject, and I was becoming uncomfortable. I was a teenager; I was in the middle of exploring my feelings about everything, as it was.

"I guess I would like to be more relaxed. Not that I'm bad at it, but I think I should be more accepting of situations, instead of trying to second guess motives."

"List three situations, or times, when you were the happiest."

I decided to be spontaneous with this question, and just utter the first thoughts that entered my head. "There was a family dinner where everyone was happy and relaxed and getting along well. Another time was when I aced a particularly difficult math test. And being with Stire is making me very happy."

Ok, that last statement just popped out. I hadn't realized how strongly I felt about our relationship. However, I didn't have a chance to mull over that for long before the next question was asked.

"What do you fear most in your life right now? Why? What would it mean if that happened?"

That was an easy question. "My greatest fear right

now regards the situation we're in. I'm afraid I'll never see my family and friends on Earth ever again."

What depressing thoughts!

There was silence for a moment.

"What specific characteristics do you want your ideal life partner to possess?"

I was a little young to be discussing life partners, but I decided to play along. *What choice do I have?*

What did I want from a life partner? I hadn't thought about this, so some improvisation was needed. "I would like someone intelligent and thoughtful; someone respectful of my feelings, but also someone that would gently point out areas I could improve upon. The operative word here is, of course, 'gently.' I would like my life partner to have a sense of humor, and be well organized." I paused for a moment. "Someone that is disorganized would drive me crazy." I stopped.

"Please continue," a voice said.

"I would like someone that has beliefs similar to mine, and someone that is playful. And that's all I have to say on the subject." I was getting tired of this.

"How do you feel about interspecies relationships?"

I had been expecting that question. "It is something that I am currently exploring."

Chapter 23

I woke up with a massive headache. In fact, my head hurt so badly that I was having trouble seeing. I kept my eyes closed while I sat up. After I opened them, I discovered I was in Reit. All around me, people were slowly waking up.

Awakening Square had plenty of room for all sixty-four of us. The fences were still down, but we had been segregated into our races, which gave me a strange feeling. After a moment, I thought I could walk steadily, so I made my way to the supply box. Stire and Frakis were already standing there, and Jana was slowly approaching.

"Well, it's nice to see everyone again," I said. "I have quite a headache, so forgive my crankiness."

Stire reached across the supply box and took my hand. "I think we all have a headache; I know I certainly do. I had a lot of intrusive questions asked of me. Did anyone else?"

Before any responses were possible, our communicators pinged.

"In one hour, food will arrive in the cookhouse. There are extra housing units available for the new arrivals. The Guardian will speak with you tomorrow morning."

"More mystery," said Frakis. "Will this never end?"

"I don't know, but let's see if there's anything in the supply box," suggested Jana.

We put our hands in the appropriate places, and the supply box opened. It contained a few supplies and a change of clothing for everyone.

Everyone gathered at the cookhouse, where we handed out the clothing.

I said, "This clothing is very welcome. I was starting to feel grungy. After we send everyone off to a housing unit, I want to go back to ours' and have a nice long shower. There should be plenty of time before dinner arrives."

"Excellent idea; we have so much to talk about," said Frakis. She updated her housing list as we organized the group.

After we took turns cleaning up, we gathered in our common room. I wasn't the only one that had been shaken by our recent experience; we all looked off-color.

"Who wants to talk about this afternoon?" I asked. "Actually, did our experience only last an afternoon?"

"Yes, it did. I checked my timepiece when I awoke," said Stire. "And I'm not really sure if I want to talk about my experience. I was asked all sorts of questions, and most of them made me uncomfortable. The subject matter wasn't really any business of our abductors. I would rather have been doing more obstacle courses." Stire was definitely sounding out of sorts.

"Which questions made you uncomfortable?" I was curious, but also cranky enough myself to not leave it alone.

"Well, the questions about emotions bothered me. For example, 'list three situations when you were the most happy' and 'how was I feeling about myself at those times?' Temmans don't normally go about thinking about how happy they are. We just exist, and then sometimes we have problems. And then there were the questions about what gods I believed in, and what was my code of conduct? The code of conduct question was fine, but the questions about gods were irritating. It was none of their business."

Stire was certainly riled, but I also thought it wouldn't hurt him to analyze and understand his reactions. As far as I could tell, Temmans had as many emotions as the rest of us.

I decided to move the spotlight. "Frakis, do you remember anything about the questions you were asked?"

"Some of my questions seemed a little unusual, considering my age. For example, I was asked questions about finance—'Do I feel peaceful or anxious in regards to money?'; 'What financial beliefs did I get from my parents?' And then there were the questions about my career. I don't really have a career yet. Oh, and the question I really hated was 'What are five of your greatest strengths?'" Her hands were fluttering about more than usual.

"It seems to me that we were all asked a different set of questions. Some of them may have been the same, but I certainly wasn't asked all of the ones you two were asked. They must have customized a list for each of us."

Jana interrupted. "Let's continue this discussion at dinner. It's time."

Entering the cookhouse, I was delighted to see our artistic endeavors from the previous evening displayed along the walls. I had been quite pleased with the mural we had created.

"Your mural is an excellent record of our experiences," said Jana. "I was hoping we would see it again."

"And I'm happy that our musical instruments weren't discarded. My drum is actually one of the better ones I have made." Stire was obviously pleased with his creation.

Our abductors were keeping us well fed. There were an amazing number of dishes. I would have liked to try some of the alien dishes, but I wasn't that brave. The seating was a little tight, as we obviously had twice the normal number of people, but it was manageable.

"So, have you made a lot of drums?" I asked Stire.

"Yes. I'm in a drumming group at home, and we make drums and then use them in our practices. I guess they still meet once a week." Stire sighed. "For me, it was a way to release tension and get some physical exercise."

Other than the current situation we were in, I hadn't

taken Stire for a stressed individual; perhaps he hid it well.

At dinner, we were sitting with the committee from the second village. The two groups were entirely different. We discussed everything; the other committee was quite silent.

"Hugo, how was your experience this afternoon?" Jana couldn't contain her curiosity.

"The whole thing left me cold. What right do our abductors have to subject us to these tortures? If I could figure out a way to get out of here, I would. And this afternoon was a farce—just a bunch of stupid questions; I didn't answer most of them."

"Do you have a plan to get everyone home?" I asked.

"I am working on a plan to get the humans home. Everyone else can figure out their own escape."

A profound silence enveloped the table for a few moments.

"Well, I appear to have finished my dinner," said Frakis. "I think I'll go outside and see what's happening."

That was just the excuse the rest of us needed.

While Stire and I were walking around the gaming area, trying to decide what to do, a Temman from the second village came up to us. We had to stop walking; he stood in our way. He poked at Stire and said, "I don't like the two of you being together; it isn't right."

"It isn't any of your business how I handle my personal life." Stire was furious.

"There are a lot of Temmans that feel the same way I do. Your relationship has become obvious to everyone; there shouldn't be any mixing of species."

"Well, that's not how the Guardian feels." It was amazing what I could make up in the spur of the moment.

I gently pulled Stire's arm. "Let's go play some Ballz." I was afraid he was going to get physical with this male Temman.

We noticed Jana soaking in the hot tub, and Frakis playing some Spider. We went over to the Ballz area and discovered a new game starting; Stire and I joined in.

After a time of throwing rocks around, Stire seemed to calm down. I could just imagine what he was throwing them at.

"Let's take a walk," I said to him after our game finished.

On our stroll, we met Frakis and Jana.

"We're going to play some Ballz. Do you want to join us?" Jana asked.

"Actually, we're going to take a walk and check out the gardens. Right, Stire?"

"Ah, sure."

"Oh…" Jana said, before Frakis interrupted her.

"You're not getting out of a game of Ballz, Jana. We have a bet on, remember?"

Jana loved the gardens. I think she wanted to join us, but Frakis was a little more tactful. We strolled along in silence.

"Stire, tell me what's bothering you." I didn't think it was the incident with the other Temman.

"What's upsetting me are the questions I was asked this afternoon. They have made me think about things that I have never had to consider."

"Like what?"

"Oh, religion, what makes me happy, and things like that."

We puttered along for a while. The sun was just beginning to set, and the flowers in the meadow had not closed for the night. I hadn't realized before what a wonderfully delicate scent came from the meadow.

Stire wasn't going to break our silence, so I decided to. "The question that really bothered me was about what I thought about inter-racial relationships. Did they ask you that one?"

Stire abruptly stopped and turned to me. He was still holding my hand. "Cyn, do you know why that question frightened me so much?" I just shook my head. "Because I hadn't understood the depth of my feelings for you." He pulled me close to him and held me tight. "I've never felt this way about anyone. I think I love you."

With tears streaming down my face I said, "That's why that question upset me so much; I feel the same way. What are we going to do?"

For a few moments, we walked slowly toward the gardens. At the creek, we rested.

"Cyn, is there a place for me in your world?"

I could have cried. "Stire, you are the center of my

life. Of course there is a place for you. Where else would you be?"

But I knew what he was really asking. "Stire, my mind boggles at all the possible directions our lives could take. Until we know how this is all going to turn out, we can't make any decisions."

Stire smiled. "I know. I'm just frustrated and frightened about our situation." He kissed me and pulled me to my feet.

Gradually, we made our way back to Reit.

We eventually fell asleep in my bed.

Chapter 24

The cookhouse this morning was home to some very somber looking people. We were all anxious about what was going to happen to us. What was the Guardian going to say?

"This waiting is killing me," said Frakis. "I had a very poor night's sleep. All sorts of possibilities about our future kept running through my mind, and not all of them were pleasant."

"I know what you mean," said Jana, moving her head. "Are we ever going to see our homes again, let alone our families and friends?"

Stire and I had very little to say. We had talked ourselves out last night, the main topic being our future together.

The cookhouse became silent when Smale arrived.

"I would like Reit's managing committee to come with me. The rest of you may return to your normal chores. Jackson and Relu will assign today's tasks for both villages." With those comments, he motioned the

An Alien Collective – Roxanne Barbour

four of us towards him. When we were within arm's reach, the dining room disappeared, and we discovered ourselves in what looked like an office.

"This is my work area," said Smale.

I looked around and saw that Smale was very high tech, or at least I thought so. I really didn't know what most of the gadgets were for.

"Where are we?" I asked.

"You are aboard my spaceship. It is in orbit around the planet. This is where I monitor what's happening in Reit, and other places." Smale pointed to a wall covered in monitors and electronic equipment.

Two views of Reit were visible on the monitors. There were other views I couldn't place, though.

"And this picture is what you would see from the window in my office at home."

We crowded around a large mural and saw tall buildings, elevated transports, and park-like areas. The transportation system and the parks seemed familiar, but the tall buildings were unusual—they were wider at the top than the bottom. I hoped they were earthquake proof—they didn't look too stable.

"Before we discuss the questions I know you have, I want everyone to take a virtual tour of our historical museum. Sit down and put these headsets on. They stimulate your mind in various ways, but mostly you will see and feel yourself walking around a museum. You will be able to touch the exhibits and, occasionally, you will be able to smell or taste items."

This is going to be strange!

An Alien Collective – Roxanne Barbour

And strange it was. We wandered through various exhibits and learned a great deal about Smale's race. We learned they were a very old race, and that they had endured their share of problems throughout their past. At one point, they had almost died off, before they were helped by another, much more advanced alien race.

The virtual tour blinked off, so I removed my headset. The first thing I noticed was Smale intently studying us. "This is the first time we have used *almost adults* in our research," he said. "And I'm not sure it has been a good idea."

"Perhaps you should enlighten us on your research. After all, we were the subjects of your experimentation. Tell us why we're here," I demanded.

"You have all made it very clear, from the beginning, that you want answers. We have now reached the point where I can start giving you some. Please help yourself to refreshments; I'll be talking for quite a while."

Beverages and snacks had appeared on the small table between us. We were sitting on couches circling it.

"You would not know this, but your four races all exist in the same arm of a galaxy. In the near future, a space anomaly will wipe out all life forms on your planets."

I couldn't believe what I was hearing. And, from the looks on the other faces, comprehension was at a minimum.

"Are you sure? All life forms on all planets?" I asked.

"Oh, yes. We have advanced un-manned science ships studying many areas of space. When this anomaly was discovered, we sent out a manned expedition to confirm the data—details like flight path, speed of the anomaly, and such. We have no doubt that this destruction will happen—and we have no way of stopping it."

There was silence for a couple of moments. I couldn't comprehend everyone I knew dying; everyone on four planets dying, actually.

Finally, Frakis asked, "What's the timeframe?"

"The anomaly will strike your planets over the course of two months. This will occur approximately two years from now. We found one empty planet that is suitable for your four races—the planet where your village resided. Unfortunately, we know of only one planet that's viable, and within a reasonable distance. All this testing has been to see if mingling your races would be feasible."

"So that's what the villages and the challenges were all about?" asked Stire.

"Yes. We needed to see which races could work together, and which ones had problems. We wouldn't spend our resources on transporting a race that couldn't work with the others. That planet would be abandoned to face the anomaly."

A little harsh!

"So what have you decided, based on the results of your testing?" asked Jana.

"The results indicate that all four races would get along, for the most part. We do have one concern, though; we only picked one age group. We didn't pick a range of ages from each race to work together. We are still considering the possibility that mixed age groups would not be conducive to harmony when all races are mixed."

"Actually, I don't think that's a problem. Teenagers are very inflexible; we think we know everything. So if we can get along, everyone can," I said. There were a few chuckles.

"Actually, the four of you, and many others, have shown great adaptability. We have been especially delighted with the actions of Reit's managing committee. You have shown us a great deal about the maturity of your races."

I believe Smale really is pleased!

"Are there other villages on that planet? Other experiments like ours?"

"No, there were only the two villages, and I was in charge of the experiment."

"What happened to the previous inhabitants of our planet?" It sounded like I was already taking possession of the planet.

"As far as we can tell, they contracted a virus that was lethal to all living beings."

"But we found some animals there," Jana protested.

"We have started to repopulate the planet with some viable food sources. What you call grak, and the fish, are proving to be successful. Actually, we had already started repopulating the animal life before we discovered your planets' predicament."

"Why did we have all those challenges?" asked Stire. He still sounded peeved.

"We needed to find out a few things about everyone. You had shown your great adaptability, but there was other information we needed to discover."

"Like what?" asked Frakis.

"Like your adroitness in dealing with others. Your ability to convince the other village to start the trek with you was very commendable."

"Even though Hugo refused?" I asked.

"Yes. We were quite astonished that he was the only one that did refuse. In such a varied group as yours, we had expected more."

The second village hadn't been a very happy place. I suspected joining the trek had been a way out for them.

"What about the other challenges?" asked Frakis. "What were they all about?"

"The train was all about practical applications. We needed to know how the races stacked up on being able to improvise and understand alien devices. Another resounding success, I might add."

Smale continued, "The maze challenge I designed myself. I wanted to see how spatial aspects differed amongst the races, and I was particularly curious as to how the group could be organized to minimize the time spent finding the red door. I was delighted with your idea of having a central group keeping track of the other groups and where they traveled. This was a novel concept, and most gratifying to me."

I really didn't think it was very novel, but letting Smale think that was fine with me.

"The lake challenge was one that combined a number of factors. For example, there were elements of working together, finding ways to solve the problem, and dealing with accidents."

"So that freak wave wasn't an accident; you created the wave yourself." Stire looked angry. After all, he had a very good reason—not being able to swim.

"Yes. Unfortunately, we hadn't realized Temmans couldn't swim. Although, if we had thought it through a little more, we should have realized that inhabitants of a desert planet wouldn't have had much opportunity to learn. Stire, we are impressed that you're trying to learn how to swim, in spite of your experience."

Smale's compliment didn't seem to cut much weight with Stire.

Smale quickly continued. "The results of the challenge regarding artistic and musical abilities surprised us; your races are so very similar in these aspects. And we were astonished at how much you accomplished in such a short time."

"Do your citizens participate in artistic endeavors?" Jana asked.

"Very little. Actually, that is incorrect; a small percentage of our race participates enthusiastically, but the majority has no interest."

Stire said, "And, of course, the obstacle courses were a test of our physical abilities."

"To a point," said Smale. "It only told us about the

physical abilities of teenagers. In addition, it revealed that you were willing to help each other. And this was very important to me."

Nothing was said for a few moments.

"Smale, what about the final challenge; all those questions everyone was asked?"

"Those questions were designed to test your self-awareness. In other words, how well do you know yourselves and your motivations?" I think he smiled. "Now, I do admit that some of those questions were unfair for young adults. You have not had enough time to experience many things. Some of the questions would be more appropriate for the adults of your species. But, what's done is done. In the end, that test helped us better understand our own testing regime—even though I do understand some of the questions were very upsetting. And Cyn-Tia, I did like your explanation of teenager—'between ager'. It explained to me that teenagers are between ages—between children and adults, and need to be dealt with a little differently."

"So, what's going to happen now?" asked Stire, ever the practical one.

"I want to discuss your different species, and then I will spell out your future." Smale took a sip of his drink.

"First let me say that each species has its own unique characteristics, but also some common ones. Temmans…"

I interrupted, "Smale, I know that we are all unique and special and all that, but what's the bottom line?

What's going to happen to us? How do we know that the spacial anomaly even exists?"

He looked at me sharply. "I will get to the 'bottom line' as Cyn asks." Smale walked over to his desk and touched a couple of buttons. "Put your headsets back on, I want to show you something."

And show us he did!

We were treated to a visual presentation that included stills of the original discovery of the spatial anomaly, and some data on the manned second expedition. Graphical representations of the path of the anomaly were shown in relation to our home worlds. The presentation even included a short clip on what would happen to life on any of the planets when the anomaly arrived. The presentation ended abruptly, and we removed our headsets.

"We have decided that you are all worthy of our attention. We will be helping the population of your four planets relocate to the planet where you were tested. The four of you, the managing committee of Rcit, will be our ambassadors; you will help us explain the situation to your leaders."

This is a lot to digest! The managing committee was lost in thought for a few moments.

"What if our leaders decide they'll solve the anomaly problem on their own?" asked Frakis.

"Bluntly, you don't have time. There is no way that any one of your planets can develop large-scale space travel, find a habitable planet, and transport everyone there in two years. You need our help."

An Alien Collective – Roxanne Barbour

"You're playing God!" I said.

"Perhaps we are, but we just want to help you survive the coming catastrophe."

That shut me up for a moment.

"What about the other sixty people here? Are they coming with us?" asked Jana.

"No, their minds will be wiped, and we will return them to their homes when we reach their planet."

"That's not fair. They have a right to remember what happened," I said.

"I understand," replied Smale, "but it isn't feasible to leave them on the planet when we are doing our ambassador tour. It's the best thing for them. There can be no argument about this."

I sighed, but it didn't make me feel any better. "Smale, we need some time alone."

"Certainly." Smale put a small object on the table. "Just push this button when you wish to talk to me."

We watched him leave his office, and close the door. No one said anything for a couple of moments. Finally, I got up, walked to the mural, and gazed at Smale's city.

Some rustling indicated that at least one person followed. This was confirmed when Stire put his arm around me.

"What are we going to do?" I asked.

"As far as I am concerned, we have no choice," said Jana. "It was fordained we would become ambassadors."

"I'm not convinced about the fordained part, but I do

think we have to go along with Smale. We need to warn our planets about the looming disaster," said Frakis.

"That part's a given," said Stire.

"Yes, but I don't like the idea of everyone else getting their memories wiped. I know I would want to remember our experience." The mind wipe definitely made me uneasy. I continued, "So it looks like we're all going to be together for a while longer." This didn't displease me.

No one responded; Stire just gave me a squeeze.

I went to the table and pressed the button.

Smale soon appeared.

"So will you be going with us?" I asked.

Smale understood the implications of my question. "Yes. It was my experiment, and I am an ambassador, in my own right."

"We do have one thing to say, Smale. We understand all sixty-four of us will be starting the trip together, and then when we reach a planet, fifteen mind-wiped teenagers will somehow be sent back to their homes, while the four of us will be in the spotlight."

Smale just looked at me, then he said, "You are correct; the mind wipe is not going to work. It would be too much of a coincidence." He seemed to zone out for a moment. "I have taken care of that matter. Anything else?"

One small victory!

"So when are we leaving?" I asked.

"Very soon. Actually, your personal items are being picked up as we speak."

An Alien Collective – Roxanne Barbour

"Well, don't forget the artistic endeavors; I want our mural along, as a record. And we need to keep our communicators."

I was suddenly feeling very sad; I didn't feel like a teenager anymore.

"So, where are we going first?" asked Stire.

ABOUT THE AUTHOR

I have been reading science fiction since about the age of eleven when I discovered *Miss Pickerell Goes to Mars* by Ellen MacGregor.

The years passed by while I had careers as a computer programmer, music teacher, insurance office administrator, and logistics coordinator for an international freight company.

I took early retirement in June 2010. Six months later, I decided to put to use all the books on writing that I had accumulated over the years, and actually start writing.

In 2011, I wrote *A Way About*, a science fiction murder mystery. In 2012, I wrote *An Alien Collective* – a science fiction young adult novel which has been acquired by Wee Creek Press to be published in January 2014.

I am just finishing my third science fiction novel: Revolutions.

For your reading pleasure, we invite you to visit our web bookstore

WEE CREEK PRESS

www.weecreekpress.com

CPSIA information can be obtained at www.ICGtesting.com
Printed in the USA
LVOW10s0307040214

372136LV00004B/9/P